# THE BLACKTHORN BRANCH

# THE BLACKTHORN BRANCH

## ELEN CALDECOTT

ANDERSEN PRESS

First published in 2022 by
Andersen Press Limited
20 Vauxhall Bridge Road, London SW1V 2SA, UK
Vijverlaan 48, 3062 HL Rotterdam, Nederland
www.andersenpress.co.uk

2 4 6 8 10 9 7 5 3 1

British Library Cataloguing in Publication Data available.

ISBN 978 1 83913 203 2

Printed and bound in Great Britain by Clays Ltd, Elcograf S.p.A.

*To Simon*

# Chapter 1

The potion was a sludgy, toady green that seemed to writhe as it was stirred. Cassie urged it, with all her might, to bubble and boil. Siân intoned the magic words, 'Hocus hokum, fix what's broken!'

Nothing happened.

Cassie lay down the stick she had been using to stir the cauldron. It dripped dolefully on the stony ground.

'Hey, careful,' Siân said. 'If you stop stirring, the magic will curdle. Do you want the spell, or don't you?' Siân glanced at the concoction and her pointed black hat slid down her forehead. She righted it with both hands. 'Well?'

Cassie did want the spell. If she could dab a drop on Byron's pillow under moonlight and change everything back to the way it had been, then she would. Quicker than a hare down a hole. Inside her cloak, she shivered. The autumn air was cold and she'd been crouching over the cauldron for some time. She took up the stick and jabbed the green juice again. She wanted the spell, for sure, but what were the chances that this mush of leaves and rabbit poos and bottle tops was going to do the trick? The plastic bucket that they were using as a cauldron sloshed as she jabbed harder. 'It's just not looking very magic,' she told Siân.

'That's because you haven't added the special, final ingredient,' Siân explained. She raised her hand and the piece of paper she was holding flapped in the breeze. It was her scrawled list of instructions for making a foolproof, cast-iron-guaranteed spell that she insisted would work.

'What's the final ingredient?' Cassie asked doubtfully.

'Two fresh nettle leaves,' Siân replied. 'And you have to pick them.'

Nettles? Siân hadn't said anything about nettles when she'd suggested this. 'I'll get stung!'

'No pain, no gain.' That was something Siân's mam said pretty often. Usually with a grim expression and her Couch to 5K app running.

'*My* pain,' Cassie pointed out.

'Well, it is *your* problem we're trying to fix,' Siân said.

That was true, at any rate.

Cassie leaned back so that her weight rested on the heels of her trainers. She looked over at the house, and her problem. She and Siân were out back, on the bit of forgotten ground behind the terrace which was half car park, half dirt track. Her house, and the friendly squish of neighbours that stretched out on either side, was right at the edge of the council estate. Right where the village met the countryside. She could see all the backyards from where she crouched — each one different, with sheds or trampolines or thwacky bamboo clumps, or

2

high mind-your-own-business fences, depending on the sort of person that lived there.

There was no sign of Mam or Dad in her own backyard. Clean washing puffed out on the line, drying in the weak sunshine. There was no sign of Byron either. Phew.

She could feel Siân staring at her. She couldn't ignore her cousin any longer. 'Are you sure it needs nettles?'

'Course I'm sure. I wrote the spell.'

The nettles grew along the edge of the dirt track, forming a spiteful hedge, higher than the wooden fence posts in places.

'Nain says nettles are good for you,' Siân said. 'They're full of iron and vitamins.'

'Yeah, when you make a soup, not when you pick them.'

Both girls stood. Cassie rustled like a crisp packet as she got up. This whole spell-casting had started when they'd filched black bin bags to go with their pointy black hats as Halloween costumes. Somehow, Siân had talked her out of trick-or-treating and into potion-making, just because Cassie had complained about Byron. She had wished that Byron could be swapped back to the Byron he used to be: part of the family, not part of the problem. She'd wished aloud to Siân and somehow that had led to her standing in front of a clump of nettles, wearing a bin bag.

Cassie eyed the jaggy edges of the leaves. They were evil. She'd wobbled and fallen off her bike into a clump of them enough times to know.

She held out her hand, fingers nipping nervously near the leaves . . . but not actually touching them.

'You're scared!' Siân said. Her eyes were bright behind her glasses with the glee of it.

'I'm not.' She was.

'You are.'

Cassie wanted to do it. She wanted to show Siân that she was brave, that she didn't mind a few stings if it gave her the potion.

But she couldn't make her hand reach out and grasp the nettle.

She felt sudden tears burn her eyes. She wasn't going to cry. She wasn't.

'This is a stupid game!' she said with a burst of anger. She turned back to the orange bucket and kicked it properly this time.

'Hey!'

The bucket rose up then bounced down with a tinny rattle of the flimsy handle and a spreading puddle of mud that had been Siân's Grand Plan. Siân glowered at Cassie. 'You didn't have to do that.'

Cassie watched the dirty water sink between the gravel, leaving tiny islands of mashed dandelion leaves behind.

'Seems there's more than one person in your house with a temper,' Siân said under her breath. She righted the orange bucket, but there was no fixing the potion.

Cassie felt her face blush hot. She hadn't meant to lash

out. But she hadn't been able to help it. Both girls were silent for a moment, stewing like potions themselves.

Cassie swivelled the tip of her trainer into the gravel, feeling the stones roll and grind like gnashed teeth. Siân had only been trying to help.

So, Cassie said, 'I'll give you a go on the good scooter.'

The good scooter had been Byron's when he was still interested in sensible things like scooters and bikes and seeing who could dam the stream and flood the bottom field the best, and not stupid, useless things like hairdos and Year Twelve girls and how to get lifts into town.

Siân clearly saw that a go on the good scooter was a peace offering — the closest Cassie would get to saying sorry.

'If you like,' Siân said.

That was the good thing about Siân. She didn't hold a grudge.

The cauldron and potion were left abandoned at the edge of the gravel car park as the girls headed to the backyard. The good scooter lived in the lean-to there, next to the no-good scooter which had come from the Lidl middle aisle and had a wheel that jammed.

But Mam was standing at the open back door. She'd looped her dark hair with a bobble to make an untidy half-ponytail. It was her why-can't-I-have-any-time-for-myself hair. She glared out at the yard.

Cassie held out her arm to stop Siân. This wasn't the moment to get noticed by Mam. There was a low wall, set with a gate, that ran along the end of the yard, separating it from the track. Cassie slipped off her pointed witch's hat and crouched behind the wall. Siân followed suit.

'Byron!' Mam yelled over her shoulder, back into the house. 'Byron! What are you doing? I asked you to bring in this washing an hour ago.' Mam sounded more tired than angry, which was worse somehow.

There was a sulky rumble, Byron's voice, but too low to be able to make out the words.

'Don't backchat. Do you want me to fetch your dad?'

Cassie flinched. Her fingertips pressed against the brickwork, as if she might be able to push her worry into the narrow cracks.

She wasn't going near the yard now, good scooter, or no good scooter. Not if Byron and Dad were about to have words. Cassie swivelled, so that her shoulder blades rested against the wall. The tail end of the sun had warmed it a little. It felt solid, dependable.

'It'll be OK,' Siân told her.

Cassie didn't reply. She looked out at the field beyond the track, beyond the estate. Her eyes rested on the green grass. The far end of the field sloped upwards and was smudged with grey thickets of autumn bramble. Atop the bramble line was the old railway track – long since abandoned and overgrown – that used to move coal and slate and people to the towns and cities beyond the valley. The field looked damp and sombre now, but in the summer Cassie and Siân had made daisy chains there and hunted for early blackberries on the slope.

'Byron!' Mam's shout was closer now. She must be in the yard. 'Forget it. I'll do it myself. But your dad will have something to say about it when I tell him. Wait . . . Where are you going? Byron, I'm talking to you.'

The gate slammed open, the wood shuddering against the brick wall. Byron stepped out, hood up, hands pocketed, his shoulders pinched high. He mumbled something, then swore loud enough for the whole terrace to hear, as far as Mrs Davies on the far end.

'Byron!' Mam shouted.

He ignored her. And the washing he'd been asked to bring in. And he ignored Cassie and Siân, watching from the lee of the wall.

'Don't you walk away!' Mam shouted at his back.

She might as well not have spoken for all the attention he paid.

Cassie felt her stomach squirm. He shouldn't ignore Mam like that. It wasn't fair. She should make *him* pick the nettles. She should *push* him into the nettles!

With his back to everyone, Byron stalked off. Not caring at all about how upset Mam was. Not caring about anyone else in the whole wide world.

Cassie stood slowly. Mam tore the sheets down from the line, pegs and all, and wrapped them round and about in a bundle. Byron stomped away in the other direction, away from the house. Cassie expected him to stay on the dirt track — it led to a footpath that ran past the junior school and to the centre of the village, which was really just the main road and a Spar shop. When Byron wanted to play at being older and grown-up and more important than he was, he'd stand outside Spar with the Year Twelves. It was stupid.

But Byron paused. He didn't go that way. He checked his watch, then turned to the fallow field and the nettle hedge. He rested his hand on a fence post and, carefully, sprung over the barbed wire.

'Where's he off?' Siân wondered.

Cassie felt her indignation burn bright inside. Byron was a lazy, thoughtless, selfish idiot. And now he was doing something strange.

There was only one thing for it.

'Let's follow him,' Cassie said.

# Chapter 2

What was Byron up to?

He had ignored Mam and nearly picked a fight with Dad, all before storming off in a mood in the wrong direction. It was as much as Cassie could do to stop herself rugby-tackling him and sitting on him until he said sorry.

'I guess we're definitely not going trick-or-treating then?' Siân asked.

Cassie untied the bin bag from around her neck and stuffed it into her hat. This felt more important somehow. 'Mam didn't even get us proper costumes from the big supermarket this year. I don't want to trick-or-treat. I want to find out where Byron's going, don't you?' There wasn't much time. Byron would soon be out of sight. 'Please, Siân?'

Siân undid her own makeshift cloak. 'Come on then,' she said.

Byron didn't look back as Cassie pressed down on the lower string of barbed wire with her foot, while simultaneously yanking hard on the upper string. Siân gingerly eased herself through the gap Cassie had forced in the fence. Cassie, who was a bit bigger and broader than her cousin, cursed when it came to her turn. 'I scratched my arm,' she said and licked the red spots of blood.

'Do you want to go back?' Siân asked.

'No.'

They followed Byron. He crossed the fallow field, keeping to the desire path worn into the grass by dog-walkers. He took rough swipes at the damp, drooping seedheads, decapitating the stems. At the end of the field, the ground rose up steeply to meet the old railway line. It had once carried the insides of the hills roundabout, out to the rest of the world, to use as coal to stoke furnaces, slate to cap homes, ore to roar and crack until the metal ran red. But the trains had stopped when Nain was a girl. Now, it was overgrown, tangled, quiet but for the sound of small brown birds tweeting their business to the sky. The old line was gone, leaving just the path to snake along the valley floor, towards Penyfro Mountain.

Byron paused for a second before starting the climb.

Cassie rubbed at her forearm, smearing her skin pink. 'What's he doing?' she muttered.

'Running away to join the circus? Looking for a ship's crew to enlist in?' Siân suggested.

'You read too many stories.'

'That's not a thing that's possible.'

Siân would read anything, from the sauce bottles at teatime to Taid's musty little book collection. Cassie still had

Christmas present books from last year that she had never even opened, so she said nothing.

Ahead, Byron was paying them no mind. He had reached the top of the old embankment. He moved out of sight.

Loose stones, gravel and burned coal riddled with holes skittered away under their feet as they climbed after him. The path wasn't kept tarmacked by the council, it was just for dog-walkers and rabbits. There was nothing up here. No reason for Byron to come this way. It didn't make sense. Cassie clung to buddleia branches and skinny roots where she could to help her scramble up. Her head popped up over the top. Taking care not to touch any of the nettles that swarmed over the sunlit spots, she pressed through to the old railway line.

There!

Byron was a figure in the distance now, moving quickly. Head down, guiltily looking like he was in the wrong place at the wrong time.

Cassie kept to the side of the path, ready to duck into a knot of brambles if he happened to look back. But he didn't. It was more like he was trying not to be seen either.

What was he playing at? The old railway line had good spots for dens in the elder and buddleia, though you had to be careful not to get scratched by the blackthorn and brambles. And there were hazel trees with nuts at the right time of year, but Byron claimed – often and loudly – that he was too old for all that sort of thing now. He had shut himself off from everyone, since Taid . . .

Cassie squished the thought before it tripped her up. She didn't want to think about that now. This was here and now, and Byron was being weird.

The only thing along this path was the old railway tunnel. Cassie had never been inside.

Even on summer days, with the sun burning hot and high in the sky, the tunnel was wet and cold and dark. The blackness slithered as you looked at it. Shifted, as though it wanted your gaze to move on and forget you'd ever seen it. In autumn and winter it was worse. Night came early and the tunnel seemed to crave dusk. Already the sun was low, catching on the uppermost branches.

Byron walked as though a tide were pulling him forwards, urging him. He didn't look left or right, he barely looked down, stumbling, once or twice, on uneven ground. He broke into a run. Not running from them, but running *towards* something.

Cassie smelled the fire before she saw it. Felt the acrid smoke making her eyes water. What was on fire up here? Should they call the fire brigade? Sometimes there were fires up on Penyfro Mountain when the bracken got dry and crisp, but it was surely too late in the year for that?

Cassie hurried forwards. As they turned a corner on the old track, she saw what was happening.

Boys. Three of them.

They'd set a small bonfire inside a rusting steel drum. The flames shimmered, rising up like letters burned to Father Christmas, twisting and snaking into the sky. Smoke, and flames and sparks of orange and white.

She stopped. She and Siân edged into the scraggly bushes beside the path to stay hidden.

Byron stood at the edge of the small group. Watching hungrily. Not a part of it yet, but clearly wanting to be.

The burning drum was set in the middle of the path. Beside it was a car. It looked old, battered, paint flaking and headlamps dirty and cracked. The tyres weren't round any more, they were misshapen, with a straight line at the bottom. The car looked like it hadn't run in years.

'Who are they?' Siân whispered.

Cassie shook her head. She had never seen these boys before. They were teenagers. One, with dirty blond hair and dirty pale skin the colour of flaking plane tree bark, held a bundle of wood, thin sticks and stouter branches foraged from the hedgerows, like someone from a fairy tale. Another stood by the car, swaying in time to music. Cassie couldn't see where the music came from.

The third danced around the fire, his light brown skin glistening with sweat, damp streaks staining his loose, white T-shirt. His hair was dark, almost black. He wore it long over his ears and it flicked back and forth as he moved. Wooden beads clattered around his neck, a wooden bangle, set with something iridescent, glinted at his wrist.

Byron stood warily, watching.

The music, a bassy, angry track that she didn't recognise, got louder. The boy danced in jerking movements – his body arguing with the beat. If a spider could dance, this is how it would do it. Cassie couldn't move an inch.

Byron stepped forwards, moving too. He was a terrible dancer. He was a terrible *everything*, Cassie thought. But that didn't stop him enjoying himself. With the yawning black mouth of the tunnel behind him, Byron threw his arms over his head and stomped to the beat.

The boy holding the bundle of sticks threw them into the drum and they caught immediately, a great roar of flame and shimmering heat. In the rising waves, Cassie was sure she saw something shift in the tunnel. The blackness writhed. It seemed that the dark bulged forwards. The boy by the fire shouted something, it sounded like an order.

A flash of blue shot out from the tunnel. It was there and gone in an instant, like the flash of a camera bulb. Cassie couldn't see for a second. The blue light had been so bright, so intense. The boys cheered loudly, delighted, it seemed, by whatever had just happened.

She blinked away the smoke and rubbed her eyes.

If there had been a black shape in the tunnel mouth, it was gone now.

She felt Siân clutch her arm, her nail tips digging into the skin. '*Ow.*'

'We have to go,' Siân hissed urgently.

'But what about . . . ?'

'Please, Cassie. We have to go. I don't like it.'

Her cousin's eyes were wide, the hazel iris almost black.

Cassie let Siân pull her away, the shouts of the boys still echoing in their ears.

# Chapter 3

Cassie stretched like a sleepy cat, feeling her muscles pop and tingle. Sometime in the night, she'd shrugged her duvet onto the floor, but she wasn't cold. The heating pipes bumped and gurgled. A warm square of autumn light spilled through the window onto her bed – she must have forgotten to close her curtains before she fell asleep. She lay starfished in sunshine, wondering what the time was – it had to be late if the sun was up – but didn't wonder enough to make her actually want to move. It was too nice and cosy.

'Byron!' Mam yelled up the stairs. 'Byron! Do you want to come with me? It's Sunday!'

Cassie pulled her pillow over her ears, hoping to muffle the morning for a while longer; whatever she'd been dreaming, it was somewhere she'd be happy to stay. But there was no muffling Mam. Seconds later, Cassie heard Mam stomp up the stairs, two at a time.

'Byron, you said you wanted to—'

Mam stopped mid-call. It was odd enough to make Cassie wriggle her head back out from under her pillow. She heard banging, rustling, the sound of Mam riffling about in Byron's room.

Then her door opened and Mam's head appeared. 'Byron isn't in here, is he?' she asked.

There was no more putting off the day. Cassie sat up and looked about with bleary eyes. She saw her chair piled high with clutter, her wardrobe with one door ajar, her floor swirled with dropped clothes. 'Why would Byron be in here?' she asked.

'He's not in his room,' Mam said, frowning.

'Perhaps he got up early?' Cassie felt fuzzy, as though her head was still half in dreams.

'When was the last time Byron got up early? He knew I was going to put flowers down for Taid this morning. He said he wanted to . . . Did you hear him come in last night?' Mam asked.

Cassie tried to wake up properly, rubbed at her face. Had she seen him come back from the railway line? She couldn't quite remember. Last night was all a bit muddled in her head. And as for Byron, she hadn't a clue. She hadn't seen hide nor hair of him in her room, that was for sure.

'Well?' Mam waited impatiently, fingers curled tight around the door.

'No. I don't know where he is.'

Mam disappeared without another word. 'Byron?' she called. The bathroom door clanged against the plastic side of the bath, the way it always did when it was opened too fast and bounced back. More stomping on the stairs as Mam decided that Byron wasn't up here.

Cassie pulled herself out of bed reluctantly. Sunday mornings were for cartoons and scrolling through clips on her tablet and maybe getting dressed at some point. They were not meant for drama. Still in her pyjamas, she went downstairs, feeling more than half asleep.

Mam and Dad were talking in the living room. She went to the kitchen and made herself some cereal.

Mam came in, holding her phone to her ear. 'No, I'm sure he's fine,' Mam said, a minute later. 'Of course. I was just wondering if Callum had seen him? OK. Yes. Yes, please.'

Cassie splashed ice cold milk onto the chocolatey rice pops and stirred it slowly with a spoon.

'When was the last time Dafydd saw him? OK. Thanks for checking.' Mam pressed another number. She'd soon run out of mams to call.

Cassie rested against the counter, spooning breakfast in slowly. Byron hadn't always been like this. Hadn't always made the lines around Mam's mouth pinch tight, made her clench and unclench her hands as she thought about him. He hadn't always made Dad wrestle with a temper he couldn't always hold down and sometimes let out in loud snaps and snarls. Even a year ago, Byron spoke in whole sentences and could make anyone laugh. But these days he was sullen and sunken into his hoodie and never looked anyone in the eye. It drove Mam spare.

Dad came in. His dark hair was tousled, standing up like dry grass. 'Any sign?' he asked.

Mam shook her head. She scrolled the names on her phone. Dad flicked on the kettle and spooned coffee granules into a mug. *World's Best Dad*, it said.

'He'll turn up. Lads do this sort of thing.'

Mam didn't bother replying. She was talking to someone she hadn't seen since Byron left Scouts. Dad sloshed hot water into the cup. The clank of the spoon sounded loud in the kitchen. Cassie slurped the chocolate milk from the bottom of her bowl then rinsed it out, her breakfast done.

Finally, Mam was quiet. 'I can't think of anyone else to try,' she said. She held her phone to her chest in both hands.

The front door opened, letting in a sudden gust of cold air that whipped down the hall and into the kitchen. 'Only me! And Siân.' Nain, Dad's mam, stepped inside. Siân, who was staying with Nain while her parents were away — on a second honeymoon, an idea that made both girls make pretend sick noises — followed behind.

Nain fussed in the hall for a second, hanging her coat over the bannister with the others. She was smiling brightly as she stepped into the kitchen. For a moment it felt as if she'd brought the sun with her. Her dark hair was fixed up, as usual, with a heavy spritz of Elnett, and her smile was made-up with the red lipstick that she always wore, even after Taid died. Especially after Taid died. That had shaken them all to the core, with Dad almost grey with grief and Byron slamming doors and yelling, but Nain had stayed firmly put-together, at least on the outside. Cassie had seen her one morning, pressing the gold lipstick tube to her lips in the hall mirror and Nain had caught her eye. 'It's not make-up,' Nain had said. 'It's war paint. With it, I'm ready for anything.' Nain was just what they needed right now.

'Morning, Mam,' Dad said. 'Kettle's just boiled.'

Nain shook her head and squeezed Mam's shoulder. 'Any news?' she asked.

'He'll be fine,' Dad said. 'He'll come wandering in, any—'

'You don't know that!' shouted Mam. 'What if he's run away? Or he's lying in a ditch somewhere?'

Dad patted the air: *All right, all right.*

'I want to go and look for him.'

'Look where?' Dad asked. 'He could be anywhere.'

'I don't know.'

They could all hear the unspilled tears in Mam's voice.

Nain looked from Mam to Dad, then back again. Not smiling so much now. 'It's quiet out. Sunday morning. Not many people about. It's perhaps not a bad idea to drive around for a bit? He won't have gone far. We won't even need to leave the village before we find him, you'll see. He'll be sitting on a bench somewhere, in a mood about something, no doubt.'

It was all the encouragement Mam needed. She was out

in the hall pulling on her shoes from the overflowing rack in seconds. 'Call me if he comes back!' she shouted.

'Wait for me,' Nain said. 'I'll come with you.' She looked back at Dad before she left the room. 'You just sit tight, all right?'

It was just Cassie and Dad now, with Siân hovering on the kitchen threshold.

Dad looked tired. The shadows under his eyes were bruised brown, the lines around his mouth scored deep in frown-furrows. Was he worried? It was hard to tell. Dad didn't give much away. Cassie got the feeling that there were a hundred thoughts all squished inside Dad's head, too many to be able to find their way out – all in each other's way. So, Dad hardly said anything most of the time. He was still in the more-grey-than-black old T-shirt that he slept in, but he had pulled on some jogging bottoms. She could see the dark blue and green tattoos that twisted up both of his arms: the name of his regiment; Mam's face when she was much younger; and Cassie and Byron's names framed by hearts.

He loved Byron, she knew, even though they rarely saw eye to eye any more.

'I'm going to tidy down here a bit.' Dad sighed. 'You two girls go on upstairs.'

Cassie was about to walk upstairs when Siân held her back. In the cramped hall, Siân leaned in close and whispered, 'Did you tell them about the boys?'

Boys?

Cassie was awake now, but some part of her brain was still dream-fuddled.

'The boys on the railway line? I thought you'd have said.'

Guilt leaped like a gas flame inside her, she could feel her face burning. She should have said, of course she should have. She just hadn't thought of it. As though what they'd seen were half a dream itself. She turned and said to Dad, 'I think I might have seen him last.'

'Where?' Dad snapped. More worried than he'd let on to Mam.

'Yesterday. On the old railway line. With some boys. They had a battered old car. They built a fire. Just outside the tunnel.'

Dad gave a clipped nod. He pulled on his trainers and headed out the back door. 'Wait here. Don't try to cook anything. Don't tell Nain or your mam that I left you by yourselves. I'll only be five minutes.' Through the window, they saw Dad cross the yard and head out the way Byron had hurried yesterday.

Would he still be there? Did he stay out all night with those boys? He must have been freezing. For the first time, Cassie felt the tiniest bit worried for her big brother.

She stayed in the hall and sat down on the bottom stair. Its carpet had been worn flat by footsteps and she could feel the hard wood beneath.

'Scooch over.'

Cassie scooched to let Siân join her. The space was narrow,

but it felt quite nice to have Siân's shoulder pressing into hers. She sat silently, letting her head lean against Siân's.

'He'll turn up,' Siân said.

Cassie said nothing. Siân didn't understand how things were, not really. She and her mam and dad got on all the time. They'd sit in their hot tub and stare at each other like they were looking at warm chocolate brownies straight from the oven. And they thought the world of Siân. She was given treats and exciting trips with school. She didn't know what it was like to live with the sadness and spikiness that had settled since Taid died. What if Byron really had run away?

Siân took Cassie's hand and laced fingers. 'He'll be fine, you'll see. He probably just went back to one of those boys' houses and stayed up late playing some daft computer game with elves in and fell asleep on the couch.'

They sat listening to the sounds of the street — the odd car driving past, a baby yelling somewhere close, even birds chirping on Mrs-Owens-across-the-way's bird table.

Then, the back door opened. Cassie heard Dad come in. Cassie swung around the stair-post as she headed back into the kitchen.

'Hi, Uncle Gareth,' Siân said.

Dad didn't say anything. He ran his hand through his hair and stood still.

Cassie could feel his anger. It was like a change in the air pressure, in the temperature, something that pressed against her skin. It was like swimming in the sea and hitting a sudden bubble of icy water.

She wished they'd stayed at the bottom of the stairs.

'This isn't the time for playing silly beggars,' he said, not looking at her.

'Dad?'

'Sending me on a wild goose chase. What was that all about?'

Cassie had no idea what Dad meant, but she could tell that he was working hard not to shout. She felt the sting of tears forming.

'There's no sign of anything up by the tunnel,' Dad snapped. 'No boys, no fire. And you couldn't get a car on the path if you tried – it's too narrow and there isn't a road. There was no car up there yesterday, was there? You were making up stories!'

Cassie felt as though her tongue was thick, her brain too slow. There *had* been a car, and a group of boys.

'We saw it,' Siân whispered. But Cassie could hear the doubt in her voice. So could Dad.

'Not you too, Siân,' he snapped. 'This is serious. Don't you understand? Serious. It's no time for mucking about.'

'We weren't . . .' Cassie tried to speak, but her voice was squeaky and she thought, if she wasn't really, really careful, that she might start crying.

'No.' Dad held up his hand. 'Don't turn on the waterworks. Just tell the truth.'

She wanted to say that she *was* telling the truth. She was! But his face was so hard, so frozen.

It was a look she'd seen so often these last few months. A shutting off, a closing down. Dad was here, but he was also a million miles away, wherever Taid had gone.

Cassie stepped back. Stepped out of the kitchen and ran up the stairs. She heard Siân behind her.

She fell onto her bed. They *had* seen a car. She wasn't lying. She wouldn't. They'd *seen* it.

But Dad was right. There was no road and the path was too narrow for a car to even get there. There was no way anyone could drive through the tunnel.

'There can't have been a car,' Cassie told Siân.

'But there was.'

'But there can't have been.'

'But we saw it.'

What was going on?

# Chapter 4

Storm Dad was still glowering downstairs. Cassie sat on her bed with her knees up under her chin, her arms wrapped around herself. She hadn't lied, she hadn't! There had been a car on the old railway line, however impossible that might be.

'They weren't boys from the village,' she told Siân, 'or from school.'

She'd played with kids on the estate her whole life and met everyone else in Penyfro Juniors. There wasn't a kid in the village she didn't know by sight, and know which part they'd had in the Year Three Nativity or know who their big sister was or what their mam and dad did for a job. Everyone knew everyone in Penyfro. It was one of the things that Auntie Sara hated, and why she'd moved across the border to England.

If the boys had been from the village, she'd know them.

So, who were they? And how did Byron know them?

She felt as though her insides were a crumpled-up sheet of paper and she had no idea how to smooth them out. It was Byron's fault. Byron and his secrets. Last year there was nothing she didn't know about him, now he'd found a whole group of boys who were a total mystery.

'I'm going to look in his room,' she told Siân.

Siân, who was sitting at the other end of Cassie's bed, gave a small start. 'Why?'

'There might be clues. I don't know. Notes from those boys, or phone numbers.'

'He'll lose it if he finds out.'

Siân was right about that. One of the surefire ways to make Byron explode like a baking soda volcano was to touch anything that belonged to him without his express — and usually reluctant — permission. Going into his room was an act of war.

'He's literally not here,' Cassie said. 'How's he going to find out?'

'Are you sure you even want to go in there? It smells.'

It did. 'It's a risk we have to take.'

'We?'

'We. You owe me for the nettle thing yesterday.' Cassie stood up, eager, now that she'd made a decision.

'It's Daniel walking into the lion's den,' Siân warned. 'Lyra walking into Mrs Coulter's flat. It's Katniss entering the arena.'

Those sounded like bad things.

Cassie crept out of her room, across the small landing, to Byron's room. The door was shut. A *Keep Out* road sign had been stuck over the white hardwood. Black and yellow crime scene tape zigzagged up and around the handle, its wasp colours warning of danger. Slowly, as if a slumbering monster might be lurking on the other side, she pushed it open.

The curtains were drawn together, plunging the room into a kind of milky gloom. Siân, creeping in behind Cassie, covered her nose. 'Ych a fi.'

She wasn't wrong. The air was practically begging on its knees for someone to open a window. Body spray fought with the reek of gym bags; oily pizza crust stench wrestled with chemical hair gel. His bed was a tangled mess of duvet.

Cassie looked around. On the hunt for clues.

His old trophies from his under-tens and under-twelves rugby games gathered dust on a shelf. Taid had taken Byron along to the rugby club every Saturday morning and had hollered his support from the sidelines. It was sad to see them so unloved.

Action figurines, some of them still in their boxes, tottered on the shelf below. They were from films Cassie had never seen or heard of. Alongside the figures, jostling for space, were completed Lego sets: ships, monsters, warriors, battlecruisers. Once upon a time, Byron would have let her look for the next piece while he consulted the booklet and clicked together the blocks. Not any more.

Everything in this room had been hoarded by Byron, everything was a secret, a clue, in its own way. A clue to who this new, more grown-up, Byron was.

'Is his phone here?' Siân asked.

It wasn't hiding in the mess of duvet or left to charge beside his bed. Cassie kicked at some of the cotton T-shirts on the floor, in case it was there.

'How about his tablet?' Siân suggested. That was on a lower shelf under his bedside table — he often watched videos or played games before he fell asleep. It was one of the things Cassie was absolutely forbidden to touch. She picked it up gingerly and swiped the screen. It asked for a PIN.

She had no idea what it was. She tried his birthday: day-day-month-month. Incorrect.

So far, she was Katniss in the lion's den for nothing. 'There *was* a car there, wasn't there?' Cassie asked. 'We didn't dream it?'

'We can't have both dreamed it,' Siân said. 'But . . .' She wrapped her hands about herself and held tight. She sat herself on the bed, ignoring the rumpled duvet.

'But what?' Cassie sat beside her.

'Do you remember getting home last night? Going to bed? It's . . . well, a bit hazy.' Siân's eyebrows scrunched as she tried to think.

Cassie put the tablet back in place. She had seen the car, and the boys dancing, for sure. Then she'd seen the glimmer of something moving in the tunnel and they'd turned to run . . . and then she'd woken up in her own bed in sunshine. No memory of trick-or-treating or eating tea or anything.

'That's weird,' she said.

'It's all weird.'

Downstairs, they heard the front door go. Both sat up – Byron?

No. Mam's voice called, 'Is he home?'

'No!' Cassie shouted back.

Cassie heard Nain's footsteps on the stairs.

'In here, Nain,' Siân said.

Nain appeared in the doorway. She looked a little less glamorous than she had an hour ago. Her dark hair straggled loose from its clip and her mascara was a bit smudged. 'How are my favourite two girls?' she asked.

'Fine.' Cassie couldn't keep the hurt she was feeling at Dad and worry about Byron out of her voice. In fact, she didn't even try to keep it out, she wanted Nain to hear it. Nain always listened.

'Oh, cariad bach,' Nain said. 'Is there room on the broom for me?' She lowered herself onto the bed and wrapped her arm around Cassie. Nain had thick arms which were wobbly at the top, she sometimes moaned about them, but there was nothing better than being pulled in by Nain's strong, soft cuddles. Cassie let herself be hugged.

'And Siân,' Nain said, holding out her other arm. Siân curled into the hug too and, for a moment, it was as though Byron's disappearance and Dad's angry disappointment were a long way away.

'We saw him last,' Cassie said, 'but Dad was right. He went and looked. There couldn't have been a car, so maybe we were wrong and the—'

'Wait, wait,' Nain said, holding up her hand. 'Deep breath. Start over. Tell me slowly.'

So, Cassie told her, with Siân adding details if Cassie forgot. Nain listened, frowning.

'And your dad found nothing there?' Nain asked.

Cassie shook her head.

From downstairs she could hear the rumble of adults talking. Mam and Dad in the living room, not the kitchen. She imagined them, talking on the couch, Dad telling Mam that Cassie had lied to him. Mam listening, just like Nain was listening upstairs. Two different versions of the same story. Downstairs they'd be wondering about trouble in school, arguments at home, wondering if Byron had run away.

Upstairs the story was about how a car could be in a place where cars couldn't be. And why Cassie and Siân couldn't remember coming home.

Two very different stories.

'You did the right thing, telling me,' Nain said.

'Where do you think he is?' Siân asked.

Nain ran her hand over Siân's cheek, teasing Siân's hair away from her face and smoothing it behind her glasses. 'He'll just have gone home with one of the boys you saw.'

'Did you see any strange boys when you were driving round?' Cassie asked.

'We didn't. We hardly saw a soul, truth be told.'

'I wonder who they were? I know all the kids in the village. At least, I thought I did.'

Nain dropped her head and sighed. 'I don't know. Byron isn't the first boy to go wandering off away from home and he won't be the last. Lost boys come home again. At least . . .' Nain trailed off.

Cassie wriggled upright, no longer caught in Nain's cwtsh. 'What? "At least" what?'

'Mam?' Dad was calling up the stairs for Nain.

Nain patted Cassie's knee and stood up. 'Don't worry, OK? Let me think about this.' She gave her warmest, cherry red smile as she left the room.

'Did you hear that?' Cassie asked.

Siân, at the other end of Byron's bed, looked doubtful. 'Hear what? She just told us to leave it to the grown-ups.'

Cassie shook her head, excited. 'She didn't, she said that Byron wasn't the first boy to go missing and Nain needed to think about it some more. She knows something!'

Cassie leaped off the bed.

'Where are you going?'

'To ask Nain what she knows!'

Siân grabbed her arm. Cassie wanted to snatch it back, but Siân's thin fingers were powerful and she held Cassie firmly. 'Wait. Your mam is upset, your dad is angry. They don't need you charging in all bull-in-a-china-shop.'

Cassie felt a lurch of pain. She was bigger than most girls in her class, but only the meanest of the mean kids ever picked on her for it. 'I'm not a bull!' she insisted.

'Not literally. It just means you go charging in without thinking,' Siân said.

Cassie pulled her arm free, and was a tiny bit satisfied when Siân staggered back onto the bed. 'Well, I won't bother Mam and Nain then. But that doesn't mean we can't do something. The grown-ups are looking in the wrong place. If they won't take us seriously, then we'll have to do it. We have to go looking for him.'

Cassie leaned so close to Siân that their faces were nearly touching. She could see the pale purple circles under Siân's eyes. 'Mam and everyone, they'll be looking in his friends' bedrooms, or under bridges or in shop doorways. They won't look in the one place they need to.'

'Where's that?' Siân whispered.

'The tunnel.'

# Chapter 5

Downstairs, Cassie could hear the grown-ups talking. They had moved to the kitchen – all important conversations happened near the kettle, after all. She grabbed her jacket from the hook by the front door and slipped out.

'Wait for me,' Siân whispered.

'Oh, you're coming then?' Cassie huffed.

'Course. Just because I think your ideas can be stupid, doesn't mean I won't do them. I'm not about to let you go looking for those weird boys on your own. I'm here for the adventure.'

'It's not an adventure,' Cassie snapped. 'Byron's missing, remember?'

Siân fell in silent step behind.

Cassie trailed her hand along the low front walls as she walked. When they were new, the houses had been identical. The council had built them like photocopies of each other. But, over the years, the people who lived there had each taken tiny little steps in different directions and the houses looked less and less like a set. Mrs-Davies-at-the-end had painted the top half of her house mint green; the Khaleeds

34

had changed their low wall for a high hedge, to stop people seeing in the front; Gemma and Tilda in the middle had added a porch and put in a rainbow window above the door. The houses weren't siblings any more, they were second cousins twice-removed.

But it was a good street, despite that. Everyone knew everyone. There was always something going on — a new baby to visit, someone getting a puppy, someone out front or out back to talk to.

Byron wouldn't have run away from this, would he? It was his home.

Cassie turned right, into the car park. Mam had a video she loved of little Byron doing his first wobbly circuit on his bike here. She looked at it sometimes, half smiling, half crying.

He couldn't have run away.

Cassie was up and over the fence. She walked faster, racing across the field towards the railway line and, she hoped, Byron.

'Byron!' she called, as she scrambled up the bramble and buddleia-tangled embankment. A magpie squawked upwards in alarm. Cassie saluted it, while trying not to slither back down.

'Wait for me,' Siân insisted.

Dad had said that there was nothing up on the railway path. No car. No way to get a car there, even if you wanted to. But there *had* been, and until she saw it with her own eyes, she didn't know what to believe. She ran fast, sports-day fast, with Siân right behind her.

The tunnel appeared up ahead.

The space in front of it was empty.

She slowed to a walk.

There was no car, no fire, no soot-stained oil drum, no over-sleeping Byron. Just the usual tangle of shrubs studded with a few crisp packets, the red washed to dull orange by the rain, dropped there months ago, no doubt. She walked slowly over the space. The bright red berries on the scrubby trees were vivid against the autumn yellow leaves. Beneath her feet tall grass grew in raggedy clumps between gravel. None of it was crushed or trampled.

This was where they had danced, wasn't it? Right there?

'He's not here,' Siân said. 'Your dad was right.'

'Clearly.' It was just stones and thin weeds and the gawping mouth of the tunnel.

The tunnel.

Siân followed her gaze. Then, walked towards it.

'Where are you going?' Cassie asked.

'Isn't it obvious?'

It was. But the sight of the tunnel was enough to bring out goosebumps, even in sunshine. Cassie had never gone further in than a few steps. Far enough to hear the *echo-echo-echo* that bounced back when you yelled inside. Like the walls themselves moaning at you. It wasn't good-scary, like the waltzers, it was just scary-scary.

'Don't you want to look?' Siân asked.

'Without a torch? Without Mam knowing where we are?'

Siân frowned. 'You were the one in such a hurry to come here. Why stop now?'

Most of Cassie wanted to say something rude and stomp off home. She didn't want anything to do with the tunnel. But a small, insistent part of her knew that Siân was right. 'OK, but just a quick look.'

They walked towards the dark entrance. The damp bricks of the archway seemed bruised and swollen. The wetness continued inside, oil splashes of iridescence shimmered on the ground. Cassie had the strangest sense that the tunnel was breathing. A soft breeze moved over her in regular bursts. It was cold and her denim jacket did nothing at all against the chill.

'I don't like it,' Siân said.

'– *it, it, it,*' the tunnel answered.

'Hush,' Cassie whispered. The tunnel shushed back.

Icy cold drops of water plooped into puddles. Beneath her trainers, things crunched as she walked.

It was getting darker as the entrance disappeared behind them. Cassie thought about reaching out to touch the tunnel wall, to keep herself from stumbling. But she had the awful sense that it would feel alive under her fingertips.

Then, Cassie realised the path was sloping down. Her feet slid forwards in her trainers as she felt the surface beneath them slant. Not stones any more, something softer, smoother. Like solid mud?

The tunnel walls narrowed. She and Siân were pushed closer together, hands held down at their sides. Then they turned a corner and Cassie realised she could see better.

Pale blue light spilled from somewhere . . . not up ahead . . . but from below. The railway path looked more like a sloping burrow leading down into the earth.

'What is this?'

'Not a railway tunnel.'

'No.'

'What do you think is down there?'

Whatever else was down there — monsters, demons, old pitheads or mine shafts — she knew, in her heart, that Byron was there. The blue-tinged, sloping passageway looked cold, the air felt frosty. Everything, everything inside Cassie told her to turn and run. Pelt back home and into bed and under the covers and hide there until morning when Byron would be sitting at the breakfast table, safe and sound with no need for any of this nonsense.

Except he wouldn't.

He had gone down here. She knew he had.

'Should we?' Siân asked.

If Byron had gone that way — and she was in no doubt that he had — there was only one possible answer to Siân's question.

'We have to,' Cassie said. 'Come on.'

Then she led the way down into the passageway, with Siân right behind.

The ground beneath her feet gave slightly as she walked; she could feel it shift to the shape of her trainers. If she stood still, would she sink? She picked up the pace. It was easier to see now, though the dim light cast shadows along the walls. The bricks had given way to more of the squelchy, squishy stuff they were walking on. Cassie didn't dare touch it. She was reminded of sea creatures, of the slugs and sea cucumbers they'd seen in an aquarium once. The whole space felt damp and cold. The throat of a dead thing, she thought.

Eventually, the path levelled off and became more cave-like, with a firm, rock floor.

The air tasted of mould and cellars. They were under the earth now. She tried not to think how deep they were, how far it was to get out again. It was too much like being buried.

And then, Cassie heard laughter.

# Chapter 6

Cassie and Siân were in an impossible, underground, deep-down world and they could hear *laughter*.

Siân whispered, 'It's only people who laugh, right? It must be a person?'

Cassie had always had a healthy respect for monsters. When she was younger she would never sleep with a foot jutting out of the duvet, for fear that a claw from under her bed would grab her ankle. Did monsters laugh? She stepped closer to her cousin.

The laughter came from up ahead. The walls of the tunnel wended left and the source of the sound was hidden behind the bend. It took everything she had to force herself to put one foot in front of the other and walk towards the laughter. But she knew Byron must be down here, and there was no way Cassie was going to let him be captured by monsters – even if he totally deserved it.

So, she moved.

The tunnel walls were dark rock, dry, and curiously lit with shimmering veins of bright blue. It was like walking down the quill of a jay feather. It might have been pretty if it wasn't so terrifying.

As they rounded the bend, her heart pounded. She edged forwards first, ahead of Siân, to see what was making the sound. For a moment, her heart leaped. Byron? Was it Byron? In the silvery, shadow-filled light, the boy-shape gave her hope. They'd found him!

But, as soon as he shifted, she saw it wasn't so. This boy was nothing like Byron. Byron was tall for his age, gangly and irritable in his own skin. His hair, when it wasn't slicked back with gloopy products, was dirty-straw blond. This boy crouched, but even low to the ground, Cassie could tell he was shorter and stockier. His hair was long, uncombed and dark as Dad's boot polish.

But, as Byron would, he stopped laughing the second he spotted Cassie.

He hissed at them and huddled over something at his feet.

Cassie stepped back, bumping into Siân.

The boy, urgent now, picked up whatever he'd been crouched over with restless hands. Cassie caught a flash of something cat-sized, but too round and greenish-coloured to be a cat. What *was* it? Before she could get a proper look, the boy dropped it into a basket and shut the lid down tight.

The boy stood up and placed the basket behind his legs,

defensively. Wait! She knew this boy. This was one of the boys she'd seen on the railway track. He'd been the one by the fire. They were a step closer to finding Byron!

'I saw you yesterday,' Cassie said. 'Where's my brother?'

The boy scratched at his ear. His fingers were dirty. There was a line of dirt in the crease of his neck. Even through her fear, Cassie recognised the sort of boy Mam would drop straight in the bath with instructions to have a good scrub in the hard-to-reach places. A boy who hadn't had someone do that for him in a long time. His clothes, too, had seen better days. His T-shirt had been white but was now yellow-grey. His shorts hung loose at the waistband and thread hung loose at the hem. Even his jewellery, the wooden beads around his neck and the bangle on his wrist had a worn, grubby look as though he never took them off.

She could almost have felt sorry for him. But then he hissed again, showing his surprisingly white teeth.

'Hey!' Siân said. 'Don't do that. We're just looking for someone.'

The boy stood, legs apart, palms wide at his hips. He was protecting something, Cassie realised. The basket? Or something else?

'You shouldn't be here,' the boy said. 'Cerwch o'ma! Eqredior!'

Cassie recognised the English and the Welsh, but not whatever the other language was.

'Na!' she told him. Not scared any more of this boy, despite the strange place she had found him. 'Not without my brother.'

'Go back, little girls,' the boy said.

Cassie hated the way he said it. As though she was stupid and small and not in the slightest bit important. It reminded her of the way Byron has been since they'd lost Taid. Hard and sharp as slate spoil. 'I'm not little. You're no more a grown-up than me.'

The boy's eyes flashed bright and a sudden sadness creased his face. His arms dropped to his sides. 'That might be true. Mwy na thebyg. It might,' he sighed. 'But you have to go home anyway. Annwn isn't for you.'

Annwn? Cassie had heard the name before, but had Siân? She was the one who always had her nose in a book, hungry for stories and adventures. Did she know about Annwn?

Siân's face was blank. At Cassie's questioning look, she gave a small I-don't-know shrug.

But Cassie knew. She'd heard the legend in school, along with tales of King Arthur and the Mabinogi. 'Annwn like the underworld? We're in the underworld? Where the tylwyth teg live?' Her lips and fingers tingled, the air felt colder, just with the thought of it.

'You shouldn't be,' the boy said. 'Turn back.'

'Byron is in the underworld?' Cassie asked. 'Caught by the tylwyth teg? Typical!'

The boy's lips twitched, the smallest hint of a smile. It was enough to make Cassie feel bolder. 'He shouldn't be here. Whatever it is he's doing. Mam's beside herself and Dad's annoyed. He should be back in his smelly bedroom, playing his stupid video games.'

Siân gripped her elbow, pulled her back slightly, and hissed in her ear, 'We're *where*, Cassie? The underworld? Like the Land of Hades? The place Odysseus went?'

Cassie had no idea what Siân was talking about. She shrugged.

But it seemed that the boy did. He stepped closer, head tilted to one side. 'What name did you say?'

'Odysseus? Hades?' Siân repeated. 'Odysseus is one of the characters in Greek myths. I read about him in the Percy Jackson books. But then he cropped up again in one of Taid's books. He's cool. Anyway, in one of the stories, Odysseus went into the underworld.'

'Odysseus,' the boy said the name as though it tasted of sunlight on water, fairground music, of being picked up and twirled around and around by someone until your feet lifted into the air. 'I remember that name,' he said.

'I don't care about Oddi-thingy,' Cassie said. 'I want to find Byron. Is he here or not?'

Siân flashed her a look that made Cassie wish she'd bitten her tongue. 'What's your name? I'm Siân, this is Cassie.'

'I'm called Twm.' His answer was distracted, apparently still savouring whatever memory the name had given him.

'You shouldn't be here. Only the people who have witnessed the rumpus dance and seen the doors open are invited. No one else can get inside. You weren't invited.'

Siân shrugged. 'I don't *think* we were invited. We just found the way in. Oh, unless . . . Is the, what did you call it, the rumpus dance? Is it you and your friends jumping about and then there's a big flash of blue light?'

'And one of the Helynt recites the ancient incantation, yes,' Twm replied.

'We were there then,' Siân said. 'We were by the tunnel with Byron. You invited us too, by mistake.'

'Helynt?' Cassie asked. 'That's the Welsh word for trouble. How can trouble recite anything?'

Twm's mouth softened again into a half smile. He dipped his head in a funny little bow. '*I* am Helynt. I am Twm of Annwn the very first and the very best of all the Helynt.'

Helynt must be what the tylwyth teg, the fairies, called themselves. Cassie whispered the word. *Helynt*. Trouble. The name suited him.

'Twm,' Siân said. 'Please can you help us find Byron? Please?'

Twm rubbed his eyes, then covered his face with his hands. Cassie could see the struggle going on inside him.

'Please,' she said as softly as she could.

He picked up the basket from the ground behind him. Turned and walked quickly. He glanced back, waved his hands. 'I shouldn't. I should send you back the way you came. She won't like it. But perhaps you are like Odysseus, with business in the Underworld. Come on,' he said. 'Though you're probably too late.'

# Chapter 7

Too late? Too late for what? What was happening to Byron?

Cassie wanted to shout out, to demand answers. But it was all she could do to keep up.

Twm moved lithely in the strange, silvery light. He carried his basket close – Cassie remembered the impression she'd had of the cat-sized creature, green-coloured – or was it more brown? – belonging to whatever was inside, but there was no more space in her brain for anything but Byron. Twm didn't look back, not once, to see if they were all right.

Was he leading them the right way? Could they trust him? It was a daft question, of course they couldn't. But there was no choice. It was follow Twm or abandon Byron.

Twm led them further down into the earth. It seemed that the place where they'd come across him was a passing place, with the walls wider apart and enough room to stretch out. Beyond that space, the tunnel narrowed again, so they had to walk in single file. Cassie kept her hands on the walls, feeling them damp and cold under her fingertips. No heat came from the seams of light. She and Siân tramped over uneven ground, sending small stones scuttering, but Twm's steps were soundless. If he got too far ahead, he'd be lost in the gloom.

'What is this place?' Siân whispered.

'You seemed to know all about it, with the Percy Jackson stuff,' Cassie replied. She didn't mind, most of the time, that her cousin knew things. But somehow she did mind about this. Perhaps because Byron was her brother, not Siân's.

'You called it something different? It wasn't the Land of Hades, like in myths?'

'Not like *Greek* myths,' Cassie bristled. 'In *Welsh* myths it's called Annwn.'

'Yes, that. I don't know what that is.'

Cassie thought about not sharing, just for a second. But there was only so much feeling alone that she could take. 'We learned about it in school. It's where the fairies live. In Welsh they're called the tylwyth teg.'

'Twm looks nothing like a fairy,' Siân observed. 'And why would Byron be here?'

'I don't know. And the tylwyth teg aren't fairies with wings and whatnot. They're people-sized. They look like people. But they trick humans in stories. And then, the humans, I don't know, die. They're monsters, really. I can't believe you don't know about them.' Her fear made her short-tempered. Her worry made her snap. She felt no better when Twm finally did stop moving and waited for them to catch up.

'Annwn,' he said. He held out one arm as though introducing them to it.

Cassie whistled as she took it in.

The narrow passageway ended abruptly. Beyond, over the threshold, was a cavern the size of a warehouse, as though the whole hill were hollow. No, not a cavern, Cassie realised that it stretched away from them. A corridor, then. An enormous corridor, a tunnel, big enough for a blue whale to swim through under yet more blue-silver streams of light. Here and there were rectangles of darkness — more tunnels like the one they had come down, opening onto this impossible space. All of the walls, from the ground right to the top of the high vaulted ceiling were covered in drawings. Thick, black marks, like charcoal, were daubed and dashed about the place. Her eye landed on stick figures and mountain ranges, birds and trees and animals all drawn with the same rough hand. One of the mountains was exactly like the collapsed-sandcastle shape of Penyfro.

'It's huge,' Siân said, after staring for a few heartbeats.

'It had to be. Once upon a time.' He slipped his arms around his basket and Cassie heard a chitter like snapping jawbones from inside.

'What's in your basket?' she asked, too curious not to ask.

'None of your business,' Twm snapped. 'Do you want to see the new boy or don't you?'

The new boy? 'You mean Byron?' Fear leaked through her like icy rain from a cracked gutter.

As though she hadn't spoken, Twm crossed the threshold. Now, a slight breeze ruffled his hair, made his T-shirt flap.

Cassie pressed her hand so firmly against the wall to hold herself up that she felt the dirt of it under her fingernails. She felt concealed in the tunnel, but in the corridor there was nowhere to hide.

Following him on reluctant feet, Cassie pulled her jacket tighter. It made little difference against the breeze.

'Aren't you cold?' Siân asked Twm.

'I'm not much of anything any more,' he said. 'What was the name you said before, the one in the underworld? I forgot it.'

'Percy Jackson?' Siân suggested.

'No, the other one.'

'Odysseus?'

'Odysseus,' Twm breathed, almost purring the name. 'It will be gone again before long, but it is so nice to have it back. He was one of my favourites, you know.'

'Favourite what?'

'I can't remember!' Twm whooped and laughed — a braying, gasping, panicked laugh that held no humour at all. It soared up, hit the high-above hard rock and tumbled back down. It was a broken-winged sound that made Cassie want to cry.

'Stop it! Stop it!' she shouted.

Twm stopped abruptly. He gave a small shrug, as if to say, *Suit yourself*. They walked for a while in silence. Cassie was almost getting used to the idea of being underground, of being in the underworld, of the stories she'd heard about unhuman creatures in the hills being real, when they passed something that made her come to a full stop. The left-hand side was punctured by an enormous arch, mirrored by a second enormous arch on the right-hand side. They were like two giant mouths yawning wide at each other.

She looked left, then right, then left again.

Both arches opened onto two more giant-hollowed spaces. But, beyond that, they couldn't have been more different.

The space on the left was filled with a maelstrom of objects. The room on the right was almost bare but for a single, solitary tree.

Left, right, left.

Siân rested her hand on the left arch and leaned inside, so Cassie followed. Nain and Taid had taken her to the city museum in Liverpool once; it had had cases and plinths teetering with curiosities. This cavern was a little like that. All kinds of things were arranged in interesting shapes, things – she realised – that had originally come from above. Columns of tin cans rose up to the ceiling, the logos old and fading. Plastic bags were woven in garlands, colourful plaits of plastic that spanned the space. There were older objects too: wooden spindles and cracked earthenware jars. Broom handles and buttons. Cupboards and car tyres. They'd been nailed and jointed and scaffolded to form staggering sculptures. They'd been turned into decorations, threaded and tied through the spokes of tyres like exploding fireworks. With a lurch, Cassie spotted an old car, rust-speckled and sagging on deflated wheels. The car she'd seen on the railway line.

'Look!' Siân pointed to a pyramid of dolls, wrapped limb around limb in a tangle of bodies. The dolls near the top were made of fading plastic in all shades of skin; further down the pyramid, the dolls were made of pale porcelain with flip-open eyelids. Right at the bottom, like dark roots, wooden and wicker dolls rotted in tattered woollen dresses. The mass of eyes stared and stared at nothing.

Above the whole array, a huge clock face ticked time. Though, Cassie realised with confusion, the enormous fingers spun and danced seemingly at random and the face was marked with seasons, not hours.

'Ych,' Siân said, still looking at the dolls.

Cassie turned her back on the rammed, ramshackle collection to look through the archway on the right.

Again, the space was huge – a giant's room with the ceiling so high Cassie couldn't even make it out.

But here, there was only one thing in the cavern: a tree so large, so gnarled, that it must be hundreds of years old. Its trunk was so thick, ten people could have held hands around it. The topmost branches were out of sight; the rest spread like gnarled fingers, in all directions. Many of its limbs were grey and bare, but she saw thorns on the branches, grown so big they could be used as handholds. A blackthorn, she realised. But one so much bigger than any she'd seen before — it was bigger than any *tree* she'd seen before. The room, as she stepped into it, smelled of long-rotted leaves, turned to dust, like a library, or an old bookshop. Only one section of the canopy had any leaves at all, and they were curled and browning. It looked ill, Cassie thought. Dying, even. How could a blackthorn grow so big down in the dark?

Her heart ached to look at it.

'What are you doing?' Twm asked them, impatiently.

'What is this space?' Siân asked, pointing at the jumble sale of stuff.

'It's the Tanglement.'

'What's it all for?'

'Reminders,' Twm said, 'of the mess people make. Gwenhidw keeps it to remind her who you lot really are.'

'And that?' Siân pointed to the opposite chamber.

'The Thorn Hall. I thought you were in a hurry?'

'Byron!' Cassie said. 'Yes! Yes, where is he?'

'Fiedown.' Twm turned away and walked ahead down the wide corridor, ignoring the open spaces on either side. 'Come if you're coming.'

So, they followed. Cassie had no idea how long they walked. Her lips felt dry, her feet ached and all the way she had the horrible feeling that there was no going back. She could see openings and fissures dotted like flies here and there all over the expanse of the corridor walls, more and more of the scrawled pictures filled every inch of space. She'd never recognise the entrance they'd come in through — never in a million years. Without Twm to show them the way back, they could be lost down here for ever. Not that she even wanted to head back without Byron.

Which meant that the only choice was to walk on.

# Chapter 8

Cassie heard their destination before she saw it: gleeful calls; full-throated yells; yelps and snarls of the rough and tumble schoolyard. Children. What Cassie could hear was the sound of children with no adult's eyes on them. In Year Five, she had been taken on a day visit to senior school and there had been a moment when she had found herself lost in the crowded corridors. It had been a noise just like this, made by boys as tall as Dad, and impossibly grown-up girls, while she shrank against the wall.

Siân took her elbow, 'Are you OK?'

Cassie nodded. She had to be. For Byron.

Twm rounded a corner and there, finally, was the end of the wide corridor, and the place Twm had called Fiedown. Cassie struggled to know where to look. There was so much, and it all cried for her attention. The chamber in front of her — because it was a chamber, though it was more human-sized than the spaces she'd seen earlier — was clearly home to the Helynt. Shaped like a house, with all the inside walls taken away, little nooks and burrows had been carved into the sides, with ropes and ladders and platforms connecting them to the ground. Children swarmed the ladders and platforms. Maybe two dozen or so. Some girls, some boys, some impossible to tell. They were a patchwork of colour and daubed with shapes, so their skin seemed tattooed. Like Twm, they wore bangles and beads and had decorated themselves with anything they could find.

Then Cassie noticed the creatures. How could she have missed them?

'What are they?' Siân whispered.

On one of the lowest platforms, half a dozen *somethings* pressed together, huddling as if for warmth. They reminded Cassie for all the world of a small flock of sheep sheltering under an oak to stay out of the rain. But these weren't sheep, they were more like beetles. Their bodies shimmered iridescent greens and mossy browns; fine fronds in paler green curled from their faces. Eyes that were nothing but black pupils blinked under the pale fringing.

'Cassie, what are they?' Siân asked again.

'Not a clue,' Cassie replied. She turned to ask Twm. But he had slipped into the current of noise with buoyant ease. Still holding his basket, he joined a knot of laughing girls. Then, as if swirling on a current Cassie could neither see nor understand, he moved on to the next ring of people. He seemed to have dropped Cassie and Siân like a stone down a well.

But he'd said he was taking them to Byron. 'Can you see Byron? Is he here?' Cassie asked Siân. She zipped herself up in courage, pulling her spine straight, and stepped into the chamber. The gaggle and cackle of voices came from every direction, even above, but no one spoke to them. The air tingled with the smell of growing roots and dry earth. Was he here? What was he doing here? She spied over shoulders, ducked under elbows, searching out his familiar, annoying, lost face.

And then, there he was.

'Byron!' Cassie gasped.

He didn't react. Alone among the boys, he sat still and quiet on the bare ground. His legs were crossed, his hands rested gently on his knees, as though he was waiting patiently for someone to read him a story.

'Byron!' When she was close enough to bellow in his ear, he finally turned to look at her.

He smiled.

It was the soft sort of smile he used to make when she barrelled into his room to tell him that the sun was up, and Mam had said it could be pancakes for breakfast. It was the smile of someone who hadn't noticed that they were deep underground, surrounded by half-wild children. 'Byron?'

'Cassie,' he said, delightedly. 'You're here too!'

'Get up.'

'It's not time yet.'

'Shut up, Byron. Don't be stupid. Get up.' Cassie tried to shove her shoulder under his arm to hoist him to standing. But he was dough-slow and refused to budge.

'What's wrong with him?' Siân asked.

'I don't know, but we have to get him out of here.'

Then the crowd moved, a ripple of head-turns, step-asides and dancing shuffles. A sudden silence. Cassie glanced to see what had changed. Someone was walking through the crowd towards them.

It was a girl. She was young, but looked older than they were. Her dark hair was pulled back from her face and tied in a messy knot. She wore earth-coloured clothes, a long rust-coloured dress and a dark wool scarf pinned across her shoulders with a matching pair of iridescent brooches and a wooden bangle on her wrist. She walked with her chin up and back rod-straight. The silence, the shuffling out of the way, was for her. It was clear that she thought herself important.

'Hello,' the girl smiled at them. 'Who are you, I wonder?'

Cassie let Byron slump back down and stood to face the newcomer. She opened her mouth to speak, but her tongue felt thick as old rope.

'Shame,' the girl said. 'You go to all the trouble to come down here uninvited and you have nothing to say.' She was taller than Cassie or Siân, and elegant in a way that Cassie knew she could never be in a month of Sundays. Her head swayed gently as she spoke. The girl leaned forwards, level with Cassie. Up close, Cassie could see that the girl's eyes, which had looked dark, dark brown, were actually black-flecked with tiny veins of blue, like the corridor walls. They had a cold, dancing light of their own, like looking at stars on a frosty night.

'I'm . . . I'm Siân,' Siân managed to croak.

'Siâni flewog,' the girl laughed. 'Little caterpillar. Yes, you don't look like a butterfly quite yet. And you?' Her face was just centimetres from Cassie's and Cassie could feel her heart *thump-thump-thumping* in her chest, telling her to get out.

'Cassie,' she whispered. 'Byron's sister.'

The girl gave an elaborate, deep curtsy and the sound of giggles swept through the crowd. 'I'm honoured to meet you. I'm Gwenhidw, leader of the Helynt, Guardian of the derew.' She rolled her palm up, gesturing to the children and the shimmering beetle creatures. Cassie frowned, Twm had called himself the first Helynt, and yet Gwenhidw was their leader. Perhaps Twm was the kind of boy who liked to make himself sound more important than he was.

'My friends call me Gwen. Are you going to be a friend, I wonder?' If a cat could talk, it might have the same lulling, watchful voice as Gwenhidw. *Gwen.* The name slipped like an innocent whisper into Cassie's thoughts. She shook herself. She didn't want to be friends with anyone who took Byron away.

'I want my brother back!' she said.

Gwen looked hurt, a line forming between her eyebrows. 'What if he doesn't want to go back? Doesn't he get a say in it?'

Byron, who had settled into his comfortable cross-legged position, just smiled absently. Cassie gave him a rough poke with the toe of her trainer.

'He doesn't want to stay here. Do you, Byron? Why would he want to stay in a manky old cave?' As soon as the words were out of her mouth, Cassie wished she could claw them out of the air and shove them back down. It was stupid, *stupid* to insult Gwen.

But Gwen didn't seem insulted. She smiled and raised her hands as if in surrender. 'Manky old cave, is it?' she asked. The Helynt, perched on platforms or peering at Cassie and Siân from close by, all laughed.

Gwen raised her hand and pointed to a wall.

One of the black charcoal drawings, a flock of birds that might have been crows or gulls, shook out their wings. The black became grey and white. Gulls, then. They swooped from the cave wall and circled above the group. Cassie followed their flight, then had to shade her eyes as she found herself peering at sun-brightened clouds. She heard the gulls shriek and, close behind, the hiss of waves on shingle. The air smelled of salt and sunscreen.

She looked down, the cave walls were gone and, in their place, was a wide sparkling beach, the sand carved in furrows beneath her feet. Three of the Helynt raced across, leaving footprints in the sand, another cartwheeled towards the sea.

Byron, who was now sitting near the tideline, laughed and let sand slip through his fingers.

'Where are we?' Cassie demanded.

'In a manky cave,' Gwen said coldly.

Gwen lowered her hand and the navy, turquoise and

cornflower blues of the sea and sky smudged and faded. The gulls cawed and clamoured before wheeling once more. As Cassie watched, they settled on an outcrop of cliff, their feathers darkened, and the cliff was cave wall. The birds, once again, were charcoal drawings down in the dark.

She'd been standing in the cave the whole time, Cassie realised. She hadn't moved a muscle. All around her, the tylwyth teg, the children of the underworld, cried out with disappointment as the beach vanished. It had been an illusion, made with magic.

Gwen crossed her arms. 'You're all taken in by a little glimmer. It's pitiful. Take him,' she snapped. 'Take him back. What do I care? I have everything I need and more.' Her cheeks flushed red, her pale pink lips were pressed white.

Cassie didn't need a second invitation. 'Byron. Move. Now.'

Together, she and Siân hoisted him up. He was as useless as an infant deer; his legs buckled under him. But they kept him up, up and moving. Away from Gwen. Out of the chamber. Back to the wide, wide corridor and the way out.

'Take him!' Gwen shouted after them. 'Take him!'

# Chapter 9

They had Byron back! Cassie could have skipped with the joy of it, if it wasn't for the fact that they were still in Annwn, with the sound of the tylwyth teg still in earshot, with no idea which of the many, many side tunnels led home to Penyfro, and with Byron staggering like a dead weight between them.

'What were you thinking?' Cassie demanded. He barely shrugged. 'How did you even meet Gwen and those boys? Do you have any idea how worried Mam and Dad have been?'

He snorted then.

'They have. Mam's beside herself and Dad's fuming. And you're wandering off into the underworld like it was just another park bench to hang out on. Byron, you're an idiot. What if you got stuck down here? What if you never got out? What if we hadn't come and rescued you? Do you want to spend the rest of your days in a cave in the dark with those weirdos and their creepy bugs?'

'Derew,' Byron said. 'They're called derew.'

'That's totally not the point!' Her words echoed up into

the darkness. It barely felt that they were moving, the corridor was so cavernous. They had to go past the two huge side chambers, she knew that — the tree in the Thorn Hall and the, what had Twm called it, the Tanglement? But then what? Which tunnel should they take to find their way home?

Siân was obviously thinking the same thing. 'If we'd been smart, we'd have unspooled a line of cotton to find our way back, or marked the right tunnel with chalk,' she said. 'Or even laid a trail of breadcrumbs, but that usually doesn't work out too well.'

They had managed to rescue Byron, but they weren't out of the woods yet, not by a long way. Cassie urged him on.

As they passed the Thorn Hall, with the ancient tree within, Cassie noticed that the patch of living leaves was smaller still than it had been. Some of the deep green leaves had dried and curled to a burnt orange and would soon fall to join the dry carpet of leaves on the ground. It was sad, the saddest thing, to see something that must once have been magnificent grow old and tired.

'Move, Byron!' she barked. 'Stop being so slow.'

His head jerked up, and, from somewhere, he gathered enough energy to break into a slow trot. It was better than nothing, she supposed.

Once the Tanglement and Thorn Hall were behind them, the corridor yawned, massive, imposing and impossibly dotted with possible routes home. There were dozens, tens of dozens of choices.

'Which is the way back to the railway tunnel?' Cassie felt cold fear drip and seep into every inch of her. She felt no euphoria. They had Byron, but Mam and Dad had lost all of them now, not just him.

'Byron, do you know the way home?' Siân asked him.

He shook his head. 'No.'

Typical.

'Should we split up? Check out a few of the tunnels and meet back here?' Siân suggested.

'There is no way we should split up. Byron will only wander off and join some other weird gang.'

Siân gave a reluctant grin. 'OK, then. In that case, we should approach this logically. What do you remember about the tunnel we came out of?'

Cassie thought back. They had chased after Twm so quickly that she had barely noticed anything about their surroundings. 'It was on the flat,' she said, at last. 'We didn't go up or down any slopes, so it has to be one of the doorways at ground level.' There were a great many openings set higher up in the walls — all of those could be ignored.

'It was narrow too,' Siân said. 'We had to walk one behind the other.' That meant they could ignore all the wide doorways. 'That still leaves half a dozen, and they all look exactly the same.'

Byron sat down on the ground, lay down, and looked up at the ribbons of blue light that threaded through the heart of the mountain. What was even wrong with him? He didn't seem to care whether they got out or not. Cassie felt her hands form fists. He didn't deserve to see Penyfro again.

'Wait! Penyfro!' she said. 'I remember! When we stepped out of the tunnel, I noticed one of the drawings close by looked like Penyfro Mountain, you know, the way the sides are all kind of slumped in some places and steep in others, and the way the top is flat? Byron, give me your phone.'

'There won't be any signal,' Siân said.

'I don't need any. I just need the torch.' She held out her hand to Byron. 'Gimme.'

He reluctantly fished in his pocket and tapped to turn on the torch. With it, Cassie ran to examine the walls. She scanned the drawings — she saw a lizard, a hawk, something that looked like a ploughed field, or perhaps corrugated metal. Where was it? She rushed to the next open tunnel mouth and scanned again. There were family scenes here, a child carried on its parent's shoulders, another being thrown in the air. No, this wasn't it. Cassie glanced back the way they'd come. Had Gwen changed her mind, was she coming after them? Then, she saw the dark scrawled shape of the mountain beside the very next opening and felt a wave of relief. 'Here!' she called to Siân. 'It's this way.'

'Cassie, you legend!' Siân wrapped her in a bear hug.

Cassie looked back at Byron. He was sitting on the ground now, his eyes turned back the way they had come, back to where they had left Gwen. 'What?' Cassie asked. 'Don't you want to come?'

'You think you've found the way out?' he asked.

'Yes, yes. Come on.'

Byron slowly got to his feet and followed Cassie into the tunnel.

# Chapter 10

The tunnel sloped up, ever so gently, once they passed the open space where they had first met Twm. The temperature dropped and the breeze pulled and tugged at their clothes. They clambered out of the burrow-mouth into the brick-lined tunnel. Cassie could almost have hugged the dripping, dark walls, she was so relieved to see them.

Not half as relieved as Mam was some ten minutes later, when they all stepped, tired, hungry and bedraggled in through the back door. She pulled them all in, calling to Dad, calling Nain on the phone to report that Nain could stop worrying too, half laughing, half crying. Hugging Byron, Siân, Cassie, and then Byron all over again.

'Where in hellfire have you been?' Dad demanded.

'What have you been doing?' Mam asked. 'You're all filthy.'

Cassie looked down at herself, at Siân's face and Byron's. They were all streaked with dirt, the scramble out of Annwn had left its mark.

'Well?' Dad asked Byron.

'I was with some boys.'

'That's not good enough, boyo. You were out all night. You've had your mam worried sick. What boys were you with?'

'You should have called us,' Mam added.

'No signal. Sorry.'

'Sorry? Is that all you've got to say after putting your mam through the wringer?'

Mam rested her hand on Dad's shoulder. 'Gareth, they all need a bath and something to eat.'

'He can't just waltz in here and expect us to say nothing, Claire,' Dad said. 'It's not on.'

Byron pulled his hood up over his head. 'I'm going to my room.'

'Too bloody right you are,' Dad yelled. 'And you'll stay there until I say different.'

'Gareth!' Mam and Dad looked at each other for a moment, holding each other's gaze and seeming to say something silently that Cassie couldn't understand.

'Take a shower first,' Dad finally said.

Byron nodded. His face looked weary beneath the dirt.

While Mam bustled about organising clean towels and spare clothes for Siân and a wet flannel when it became clear Byron wasn't getting out of the shower anytime soon, Dad pulled Cassie aside. 'I'm sorry,' he said softly. 'I didn't mean to shout at you earlier. It was the wrong time for you to play games. But I shouldn't have lost my temper.'

*Play games?*

Of course. Dad thought she'd been lying about seeing Byron on the railway line. He was never going to believe the rest of it. Why would he? How could he? It sounded like the biggest, fattest lie anyone had ever told. Byron had been whisked away to the underworld by a girl-who-wasn't-a-girl called Gwen? That there were caverns under the mountain that weren't just abandoned mines and railway tunnels? That an enormous blackthorn tree grew in the dark and, with just a wave of her hand Gwen could conjure the swell of the sea down in the pit of the earth?

Magic, she realised, she was talking about magic. And, in the kitchen thrumming with the soft hum of the fridge, under the spotlights Dad had installed, beside the biscuit jar and bottle of Fairy liquid and the draining board, and all the other hundred and one ordinary things, there was no room for magic.

Mam stepped in, her eyes shining. 'I've not done anything for tea. And it's a Sunday too. No roast!' Sunday was usually the best meal of the week, when there would be roast potatoes and roast parsnips and gravy and peas, and everyone would squish in around the living room table to eat. Or they used to at least. Taid wasn't there any more, and Byron was out with friends, more often than not.

'Fish supper,' Dad said. 'I'll go to the chippy and we can all have something nice. How's that?'

'Perfect,' Mam said.

'And then,' Dad said, 'Byron can give us a proper explanation of where he's been.'

Cassie couldn't help but wonder how Byron was going to do that.

As it turned out, Byron didn't even try to explain himself. Dad had delivered Siân back safely to Nain's house and come home past the chippy with all their favourites: chips slathered in salt and vinegar, steaming inside the paper wrappers, crisp battered fish and small pots of curry, gravy and mushy peas. He had laid it out on the plates that Mam had warmed in the oven. And Byron didn't come down to eat any of it.

'He's a teenager,' Mam said. 'What do you expect?'

'A bit of respect wouldn't hurt. My dad wouldn't have stood for it, I can tell you.'

'Your dad would've . . .'

'What?'

'Nothing.' Mam speared the last of her chips and dunked them in red sauce.

When tea was done, Dad sorted out the empty wrappers and the washing-up. So, Cassie headed upstairs.

Byron's door was closed. She tapped on it, gently.

'Go away,' Byron said.

She pushed it open. The curtains were drawn and there was no light on, not even from his tablet. Byron was curled up, in the dark.

'Are you all right?' she asked.

He said nothing, so she stepped closer. There were a hundred questions in her head: how had he found his way

70

to Annwn? How had he met Twm and the others? What had happened yesterday that meant he hadn't come home? Was it over? That was the big one. 'Are you safe?' she asked.

Byron rolled over to face her. 'This is none of your business, Cassie,' he said. 'You're just a little kid. Stay out of it, yeah?'

'But—'

'I mean it. Now get out.'

Cassie backed out, and, in the narrow shaft of light cast into the room from the landing, she could have sworn that she saw a flash of blue light sparkle for a moment in Byron's brown eyes.

# Chapter 11

Cassie lay in bed, the room was mostly dark. An orange wedge of streetlight seeped in where the curtains weren't pulled tight – it looked like a knife blade cutting the ceiling. She couldn't sleep. She just didn't feel tired, not one little, teensy bit. The worn-down fur of her teddy bear, usually reassuring and cosy, gave her no comfort as she cuddled up to it in the dark.

Had Byron's eyes been streaked with blue, just for a moment? Or had she imagined it? Was it just tiredness after the strangest day imaginable? It had to be. Gwen had let them leave, had practically pushed Byron out of Annwn.

It was over, right? She pressed her face into Mr Tibbles and tried not to think of Gwenhidw and the tylwyth teg.

It was all she could do to get through school the next day. Her mind was pulled back and back to Byron. Mrs Khaleed noticed and asked if she was feeling OK. It wasn't like Cassie to be so quiet. 'Wyt ti eisio i mi galw Mam?' she asked at dinnertime, but Cassie shook her head – she didn't want Mam called, she'd only be worried.

There was only one person she wanted to see when she felt so churned up, and that was Nain.

As soon as the bell went for the end of day, she rushed out and, instead of heading home, headed straight up the hill.

Nain's little house was in one of the rows of squat red terraces that striped across the slopes of Penyfro Mountain. Above her head, the sky was a watery, seal-skin grey, the sun only just peeping over the mountains that formed the other side of the valley. The dark shape of the old pine plantation on the opposite slope looked like a gravy stain on a green tablecloth. From the valley floor, where the council estate and junior school were, it was all uphill to Nain's. The old allt road narrowed, with passing places for the farm tractors that still ran, smelling of cooking oil and burned bread. As Cassie climbed, she wondered what Twm and Gwen were up to in the cavern beneath her feet. She hoped to never, ever, ever see them again.

She was warm by the time she reached Nain's house. The light was on in the front door, casting a glow over the red-brick wall. There was no front garden, not even a pocket to put the bins on, so Cassie could see right inside, where the net curtains didn't quite meet the sill. Nain was sitting on her comfy chair, a cup cradled in her hands. She stared at the fireplace, the empty grate. Just sitting.

During the day, the front door was often on the latch, but Nain locked everything up as evening came on. Cassie knocked and waited.

'I wondered if you'd turn up,' Nain said as she opened the door. 'Come on in, it's cold out there.' Nain pulled her into a hug. Her arms felt strong around Cassie's back. She could lean into Nain and the smell of her perfume, and all the world was all right for a while. 'There now. Never too old for a hug,' Nain said cheerfully.

Inside was cosy. The sturdy walls kept out the cold, and something of Cassie's fears. She felt able to breathe better in Nain's house, her shoulders rested that little bit lower.

Cassie kicked off her boots and waded through the thick carpet into the front room. Now that she was here, she couldn't think of any sensible way to tell Nain what she'd seen. Where she'd *been*.

'I'll see where Siân is and put the kettle on,' Nain said and left Cassie to make herself at home.

Moments later, Siân clattered down the stairs. Her school in England had a different half term, so she had the week off. Cassie wondered what she'd been up to today. Then, she noticed the small bundle of books in Siân's hands.

'What have you got there?' Cassie asked. If she had a day free, with no one telling her what to do, she would be damming the small stream to make a pond or doing one of those 'make your own necklace kits', not reading the books in Nain's house.

'I found *Welsh Fairy Tales, Myths and Legends* and *The Wanderings of Odysseus* and *Black Ships Before Troy* on Taid's old bookcase,' Siân said. 'Did he ever read them to you?'

Cassie snorted.

'You don't know what you're missing,' Siân shrugged.

'Does Nain know why you're reading them?' Cassie asked.

Siân shook her head. 'I didn't want her looking at me like Uncle Gareth did, thinking I was telling lies. And anyway, we got Byron back, so it can just be a weird thing that happened that's all over now.' Siân dropped down onto the couch and spread the books onto the seat next to her. 'I'm going to read that one next.' She pointed to *Welsh Fairy Tales, Myths and Legends.*

'About Byron—'

'Here we go!' Nain sailed into the room carrying a tray spread with teacups and a small plate of biscuits — pink wafers, which weren't the best kind, but were better than plain digestives so Cassie took one happily.

Once they'd all taken what they wanted, Nain sat down heavily on her pouffy chair. The teacup resting on the arm wobbled in its saucer. Cassie sat on the couch across from the dark grate. She pulled a crochet blanket off the back and cuddled it about herself. On the mantle was an old photo of Nain and Taid when they'd just got married and Nain's hair was still black as coal, without the help of a box, and woven with white flowers.

Cassie stared at the photo of Taid in his good suit, with a funny goatee beard and his chunky watch on his skinny wrist — Byron owned that now. Dad had given it to him on one of the days when he was trying to get along. Not for the first time, she wished Taid was still around. He'd been Byron's rock, and Dad's too. Without him, they were both so lost. Byron even more so now.

Siân thought Byron was safe. But Cassie couldn't relax. She was half sure his eyes had looked strange last night, and there was just a horrible, crawling sensation in her tummy that told her something was wrong.

It was time to let Nain know what was going on, even if she did look at them the way Dad had.

'So,' Nain said, 'you're more crumpled up than a used tissue. What's the matter? Aren't you pleased Byron's back safe?'

'But he's not back safe, Nain,' Cassie replied. 'I don't think any of us are. I know you probably won't believe me. He was somewhere bad. The boys I saw him with . . . I know how it sounds, but . . . they live under the mountain.'

'Under it?'

Siân nodded. 'It's true!'

'Right under it,' Cassie continued. 'Like Alice, but the rabbit hole is the railway tunnel. There's a girl there. Gwen, Gwenhidw. She's like a witch or something. A tylwyth teg. She said she let him go. But I don't think she did, not really. I'm not making it up, I promise I'm not.' It all came out in a rush. Cassie twisted the crochet blanket in her fists, feeling the wool squeak. 'She had Byron. He wanted to be there. But she let him leave with us when we asked. And I don't know why.'

There was silence for a while. Nain didn't reach for her tea and all Cassie could hear was the whistle of the wind in the chimney and the heavy tick-tick-tick of the clock.

'Why don't you tell me all that again, but this time a bit slower?' Nain asked.

So, Cassie did. Every single thing she and Siân had seen or heard over the last few days. Siân chipped in when Cassie forgot something or didn't explain it the way Siân would have. They told Nain about meeting Twm and seeing the Tanglement. They told her about the enormous, impossible blackthorn tree and the derew, the strange creatures that lived in Fiedown with the Helynt. And they told her about Gwenhidw.

Nain sighed slowly, blowing all the air right from the bottom of her lungs. 'So, you saw the tylwyth teg, did you?'

For a panicked moment, Cassie wondered if Nain was teasing them. 'You do believe us, don't you?'

Nain nodded. 'I do. I wish I didn't, but I do. I grew up in Penyfro, remember, and Byron isn't the first person to find his way into the old places through the cracks in the earth.'

Cassie's heart leaped a hurdle in her chest. 'You've seen Annwn too?'

'No, not me. But a boy in Taid's year at school. He did. Or he said he did.'

Nain stood up and walked over to the mantelpiece. She picked up the framed photo of herself and Taid when they were so young. She stared at it for a while. Then, she spoke,

'It made your taid sad for a long time. His friend, Alun Wyn Roberts, his name was, had grown up in the village. They went to the same chapel. One day Alun Wyn came to school, full of himself, full of stories of Annwn and the tylwyth teg. Everyone laughed, of course. Even your taid. He felt terrible about that. Because a week after, Alun Wyn disappeared. Some people thought he'd run away, what with the teasing and everything. Gone to Liverpool, or Manchester, one of the big cities. But your taid was never so sure. He went out with the search parties. They combed Penyfro Mountain. Worried he'd fallen in a mine shaft or something. But there was no sign.'

Nain put the photo back, adjusted it a bit to make it line up with the others. 'That's when Taid started getting interested in myths and legends. I'd try to get him to read some of my crime and thrillers, but it was the old stories he liked.' Nain laughed sadly. She turned and picked up one of the books Siân had brought down, *Black Ships Before Troy;* she stroked the cover softly, running the tips of her fingers over the gold circle embossed on its cover. 'He loved this one. He liked to read it to Gareth and Sara when they were little.' Nain stood for a moment, holding the book, lost in her memories.

But something was bothering Cassie, a panicky something that made it hard to breathe all the way down. 'Nain, if Alun Wyn told Taid that he'd seen the tylwyth teg,' she said, 'and he disappeared a week later, then Gwen must have let him go for a while. Alun Wyn must have thought he was free. But Gwen snatched him in the end.'

Nain put the book back on the couch with a sigh. 'I suppose perhaps she did, yes.'

Cassie recalled the sudden flash of blue she'd thought she'd seen in Byron's eyes last night. It had to be a trick of the light. That's all it was. It had to be.

'What happened to Alun Wyn?' Siân asked.

Nain shook her head. 'I don't know. Over time, people stopped looking. Then, when there was no letter, no news at all, people assumed he must have had an accident and died out on the mountains.'

'Do you think the tylwyth teg killed him?' Cassie whispered.

'What can we do?' Siân asked.

Nain looked at her sharply. 'You'll do nothing. You and Cassie and Byron are to stay as far away from that tunnel as is humanly possible.' Nain turned away from the fireplace and ushered Cassie and Siân out into the hall. She pulled on her puffy gardening jacket and boots, then opened the front door onto the cold of the early evening. 'I, on the other hand, am going to do something for you. Come!'

Together they stomped out of the house. In moments, they left the street behind, as Nain led them both up a narrow footpath, overgrown with buddleia and bramble. Only dog-walkers came this way — it was a shortcut up to the top of the mountain.

'Nain, what are we doing?'

The only reply Cassie got was Nain waving at her. Not helpful.

Once the path cleared the houses, it widened out and the shrubby undergrowth grew sparser as they reached the point where sheep grazed the close-cropped grass. The wind was biting, and Cassie saw Nain's ears were a pinched red, to match her lipstick. The first stars were out, diamond-pink against the navy of evening. From here she could see the roofs of the old village on the slope below, smoke puffing from some of the chimneys, then, on the valley floor, the neat grid of streetlights that marked out the council estate. What were they doing on the mountain in the dark?

Nain stopped walking suddenly and spun around, as if she were looking for someone.

'Gwen isn't up here,' Cassie said, 'she's down, down, down there.' She pointed to the ground under her feet. Beneath the thin soil cover, beneath the rock below, deep, deep down into the belly of the mountain, that's where Gwen was. Not up here.

'Cassie! Siân!' Nain called from beneath a slender tree. Its leaves were pale — in daylight they might have been yellow — and dark berries clustered in clumps across its branches. Nain rested her palm on the trunk of the tree, as though it were the shoulder of an old friend. 'This is rowan. Do you know it?'

Cassie shrugged. It wasn't a tree that was good for making a den and its berries were only any good for the birds.

'Rowan?' Siân repeated.

'Sometimes called mountain ash. You can recognise it because its leaves look like a zip. See?' Nain added.

Siân shook her head, 'I only know rowan as a girl's name.'

Nain finally chuckled, despite the seriousness of the situation. 'My nain would be spinning in her grave. She was a proper farm girl. She knew all the old names for the flowers and birds and trees. She taught me when I was your age.'

'Well, you should teach us then,' Siân said.

'Cheeky monkey. What do you think I'm doing?'

Cassie thought about the tree down in Annwn. She saw its twisted branches with their dagger thorns. 'Did your nain ever tell you anything about blackthorn trees?' she asked.

It was hard to read Nain's face, she looked mostly worried and a bit sad, but there was something else too, as she remembered her own grandmother. 'She didn't have a lot of love for blackthorn, despite the sloes. Witches used to make their brooms from its branches.'

Witches? *Witches?*

Nain took a pair of secateurs from the pocket of her puffy jacket. She held them like scissors in one hand, while, with the other she flexed and bent the lower branches of the rowan. When she found one she was happy with she snipped a short section free and trimmed the leaves from either side of the central stem.

Cassie didn't ask what she was doing. Nain was working on a plan, and that was good enough for her.

Nain cut the thin wand into three sections. She took the first section and wound the two ends with garden wire from another pocket. She'd made a bracelet. She made two more quickly. Cassie jigged from one foot to the other, impatient now.

'Here, put this on.' She handed the middle-sized bracelet to Cassie. A second one, she gave to Siân.

'Who's the other one for?'

'Byron. I'm not having the tylwyth teg come near any of my grandchildren, not if I can help it.' Nain sounded so sure, so determined. Cassie pulled on the wooden bracelet, shoving her jacket cuff out of the way to get it on properly.

'Will this work?' Siân asked.

Nain wiped the blade of her secateurs on a tissue she pulled from her sleeve, then popped them back in her pocket. 'According to my nain, God bless her soul, all magical or ghostly creatures hate the wood of the rowan tree. It's like poison. It will protect you. If my nain's right.'

Cassie held her wrist. The bracelet felt very flimsy.

'What if she isn't?' Siân asked.

'My nain was never wrong. Except about betting on the horses. She was always wrong about that. Come on, let's get back indoors. It's freezing.'

Cassie took the bracelet for Byron and followed Nain back down Penyfro Mountain.

# Chapter 12

Cassie left Nain's a while later with the rowan bracelet firmly around her wrist and another just like it in her jacket pocket.

'Do you want me to come with you?' Siân asked.

Cassie shook her head. Nain had given her a way to protect Byron, in case Gwen really was still after him. It would be easy enough to get him to wear the bracelet, she didn't need Siân's help with that. 'It's fine,' she told Siân. 'There's nothing to worry about, anyway, I'm sure. Gwen let Byron go. You heard her. I'm probably imagining things.'

'But what about Alun Wyn?' Siân dropped her head to one side, full of sympathy.

Cassie had absolutely no room for her cousin's sympathy. 'Alun Wyn was probably a whole lot more interesting than Byron. I mean, look at the state of Byron. And Nain's bracelet will keep him safe. Not that he's in any danger. None of us are,' she said firmly.

'Well,' Siân said, 'if you're sure. I'm going to carry on reading, though. Just in case there's any clues in the legends.'

Cassie wanted to tell Siân to leave it, to forget about what they'd seen and just never take off the bracelets and let that be that. But she was scared that Siân might say they did have reasons to worry, so she said nothing.

Cassie walked back down the allt towards the main road that ran through the village. She passed a dog tied to a display board outside Spar. It sat obediently next to the lottery advert. A few cars pulled past. An old man in a Wales rugby top and worn-down trainers gave her a small nod as they crossed on the pavement. Everything was normal.

It was normal.

She pressed her fingertips against the bracelet in her pocket.

Everything was normal and safe and boring again.

And, if it wasn't, then the bracelet would fix it.


Mam was at home, but there was no sign of Dad. Byron was still up in his room. That wasn't odd, one of the things that he and Dad rowed about so often was the amount of lounging and sleeping Byron did. What was odd was the way Mam hovered near the bottom of the stairs, not going up, but not leaving it be either; she seemed nervous in her own house.

'What are you doing?' Cassie asked as she tried to wodge her jacket onto a hook that already had two other coats on it.

Mam took the jacket from Cassie's hand and hung it from the loop at its collar. 'I was thinking about getting a cup of tea for Byron, but I don't want to wake him if he's asleep.'

'Why would he be asleep?' It was only just dark, way too early for bed.

'I haven't heard him in a while and he looked exhausted when he came home.'

'He's probably just got his earbuds in.' Cassie tried to sound cheerful, but there was a lump in her throat that she couldn't dislodge. She reached for her jacket pocket and pulled out the bracelet.

'What've you got there?' Mam asked.

'Just something for Byron. To cheer him up.'

Mam dropped both her hands onto Cassie's shoulders and pulled her into a cuddle. 'You're a good one, you are,' Mam said. 'Making presents for your brother.'

Cassie let herself lean on Mam. It would be so nice to tell her what was going on. But she was too like Dad; she was too no-nonsense. Mam liked to deal with problems she could touch: leaky taps, broken lightbulbs, torn clothes. She said there was no need to go looking for trouble, trouble came looking for you often enough. There was no way she would believe that creatures from fairy stories were interested in Byron. Nevertheless, the words wavered, waiting, behind Cassie's teeth. Then Mam said, 'It's hard for you to understand, Cassie. He's a teenager. He has all these hormones and feelings rushing through him like cars on a Formula One track. It must be difficult, seeing him grow away from you?'

That wasn't it. That wasn't it, at all! Cassie pulled away from Mam's hug. 'I've got to give him this.'

'OK. But don't wake him if he's asleep. And, if he's awake, ask him if he's hungry, or wants a cuppa, would you?'

Cassie climbed the stairs with Nain's little circle of magic clutched tight in her hands.

Byron was awake. Sort of.

Cassie pushed open his door, expecting the usual explosion of fury, but Byron was silent. He was perched on the end of his bed, in a crumpled T-shirt and faded jogging bottoms, with his hands on his knees. For once, his curtains were open, and he looked out onto the dark street with the glowing cinder toffee-coloured lamplight. What was he looking at? Cassie crept into the room, she could see herself reflected back twice in the double-glazing, but she couldn't see anything that might have caught Byron's rapt attention.

'Byron?' she whispered.

All day she'd been telling herself that it was fine. She'd told herself that they'd convinced Gwen to let Byron go and that was the end of it. She felt her eyes sting, then dashed the tears away angrily. Mam was right, all teenagers were like this. There was nothing at all to worry about.

'Byron, what are you doing?'

'Watching the moon rise,' he said.

'The moon?'

He gestured. Outside, she could see the bone-white crescent hanging just above Mrs-Owens-across-the-way's roof.

'Why?'

'Why not?'

'Mam's worried about you,' Cassie said. She wished she could sit down, drop to the floor and tip out a box of crayons, or Lego, the way she used to do. But Byron's face was so cold, so blank, it was impossible. 'I've got something to help.'

He turned away from the scattering of stars to look at her. 'Help with what?'

Cassie held out the bracelet of rowan wood with both hands, an offering.

Byron frowned, confused. 'Help with what, Cassie?'

'You're not OK, are you?'

'What are you going on about?'

'Just put it on, would you?' Cassie snapped. She stepped closer, still holding the bracelet out like one of the wise men at Nativity holding out gifts.

Byron's face creased into something like disgust. 'What is it? It's manky.'

'Put it on!' she insisted.

She moved right up to him, grabbed for his wrist. He swayed and pulled back. He was bigger than her, stronger, he always had been. But, right now, he moved slowly, as though the message to move took too long to get from his brain to his arm. Cassie was quick and she was determined. She manacled his wrist with her fingers, holding tight for grim death. With her other hand she forced the bracelet over his thin, pale fingers.

The bracelet dropped onto his wrist, a hoop dropping onto a pole like some children's game.

For a split second, it rested there against the dark hair of his forearm. His eyes locked with hers. And Cassie saw the unmistakable swirl of blue light flood his irises.

'No,' Cassie whispered. She pressed the bracelet down further, indenting it into his skin. 'No!'

'Get it off!' Byron lurched up to standing. He clawed at his arm. His face was twisted in pain and revulsion. 'Get it off me.' His fingernails scratched at his own skin. Red lines bloomed. The bracelet shot off his arm and flew across the room, bouncing off the far wall. 'Get out! Get out!' Byron yelled.

'Cassie!' Mam was at the door. 'What in God's name are you doing to your brother? Out! Leave him be.' Mam was furious. She pointed downstairs, her arm rigid as a signpost.

Cassie's heart was pounding, breaking her chest. Despite that, she crept out of the room without a word. But, before she left, she bent down and scooped up the bracelet that had been supposed to help.

# Chapter 13

There was no doubt, no doubt at all. Gwenhidw had let Byron walk out of Annwn, but she hadn't let him leave. She was playing some horrible game of cat and mouse with him. Why?

Cassie lay awake, staring at her grey ceiling, Mr Tibbles tucked into the crook of her neck to try to make her feel calmer, but there was no calming her brain. It raced in tight circles, her heart still galloped in her chest.

She got up, wandered downstairs and absent-mindedly took a cheese slice from the fridge. She took it back to bed and nibbled at the square, her teeth moving along its edge like an old-fashioned typewriter. It helped her to think.

Whatever it was that lit Annwn was inside Byron too. The magic of the underworld had got into him somehow.

What had he done?

What stupid thing had he done to make it happen?

And what could she do to make it stop?

What could she *do*?

With the cheese wrapper discarded, with both bracelets

firmly on her wrist, and with the questions drumming in her mind, she finally fell into a restless sleep.

School was the last thing she needed. What was the use of fractions when your big brother was being sucked into the underworld by an ancient monster?

She got dressed in her uniform, tugged a brush through her hair, but it was impossible to think of anything but the flash of blue she'd seen in Byron's eyes and the awful way he'd clawed at his wrist – as if the bracelet burned.

Breakfast was its usual rushed affair, with Mam hunting out bags and shoes and keys with half a slice of toast going cold in one hand. Dad searched the basket of clean laundry for a shirt he could iron.

'I want Byron to walk me to school today,' Cassie announced.

'What?' Dad fiddled with the plug, trying to get the cord untangled from the legs of the ironing board.

'You're busy. Byron can do it.'

'Is he even awake?' Mam asked.

Dad gave a small grunt. 'Well, if he isn't, he blinking should be. If he gets up now he'll have time to walk you to school before he gets the bus. It's a good idea. He should pull his weight more. Especially after that stunt he pulled the other night.' He crossed the living room and yelled up the stairs, 'Byron! You're walking your sister to school. Rise and shine.'

It took Cassie standing over him and rolling him back and forth like he was Play-Doh to get him to open his eyes.

'Get off!' he groaned.

'You're walking me to school before you get the bus.'

'I'm on study leave.'

'No, you're not, your exams aren't for ages. We have to go in exactly thirteen minutes,' Cassie told him. 'Put a jumper on, it's cold out.'

She hadn't known if he would do it. She wasn't sure how or when it had become such a big thing to ask him to go anywhere with her. Once, he would have loved to walk her to school, to make sure she walked on the inside of the pavement to stay safe, to wave her off as she rushed into the Year Two classroom. That Byron was long gone.

But, in closer to twenty minutes, Byron was up, dressed and outside the house with her. Grunting his answers, hands shoved into his pockets, but outside.

The fresh breeze, the early winter chill, gave her an idea. 'I don't want to go straight to school,' she said. 'Text reception, say I'm going to be late.'

'Why? If I'd have known you wanted to be late, I could have had an extra ten minutes in bed.'

'Please?'

He shrugged. *As if I care,* the shrug said. But he got out his phone and pinged a message.

'Walk up the mountain with me,' Cassie said.

Byron faltered, paused, before walking on.

Cassie understood why. A good walk had been Taid's solution to everything. Feeling down in the dumps? A good walk. Trouble at school? A good walk. Feeling grumpy at the world? A good walk.

His favourite walk of all was to climb, red-faced and panting, to the top of Penyfro Mountain and feel the rush of the wind, uninterrupted as it flowed across the land. To taste the heather tang and feel your hair lifted up and tousled. Every Sunday, Dad and Taid would walk up the hill to the moor and watch the sky. They'd see the fighter jets flying so low you could almost wave to the practising pilots; they'd watch hawks of all kinds, kestrels and buzzards and even red kites, riding the thermal winds above the valley. Taid used to say that there was nothing like a steep walk to clear out the cobwebs.

Cassie was inviting Byron to blow the cobwebs away, the way Taid would have done.

Byron looked from the footpath to the grey railings and the road beyond where early morning school traffic nudged bumper-to-bumper, making the air taste tired and used.

'Walk with me,' she said again.

He gave a tiny nod. So, feeling like she'd won a small battle, Cassie led the way: past the school with the yells and constant motion of the yard, to the main street and up the allt, past Nain's house and the other terraced houses cwtshed into the mountainside.

The climb was too steep for talking, but Cassie could think

of nothing to say that wasn't everything all at once, so the breathlessness didn't matter. The pavement turned to footpath soon enough, a mix of freezing mud and planes of hard slate. After a while, she unbuttoned her jacket. On walks with Taid, she might have lifted the hem of her jacket up over her head, turning it into a sail against the wind, but that didn't feel right today.

They passed the copse of rowan, but Cassie said nothing, let Byron steer a wide berth around them.

Then, they were at the summit.

There was no further to climb, so they had to stop and stand, on the top of the world — or at least the top of their small part of it. Penyfro was the tallest of the foothills that led eventually to the dramatic peaks of Eryri — Snowdonia — in the west. The mountains were the teeth of the earth, with their peaks snow-white in winter. The lazy river, on the valley floor, cut through fields and behind houses, twinkling in the low sun.

Cassie wanted to ask Byron so much. The questions were backed-up, like the traffic outside school: how had he met those boys? How had he met Gwen? What had he done to make the magic take root inside him? And, most importantly, was she going to lose him like Alun Wyn's family had lost their boy? Like she'd lost Taid?

He stood near the edge, his back to her. The wind was fierce, *bracing*, Nain would call it. He almost seemed to lean into it, though of course, it couldn't take his weight. Byron took his hands from his pockets and raised them above his head. The cuffs of his jacket dropped, and his bare wrists and narrow fingers reached towards the sky. With a pang, Cassie saw the scratches he'd made himself, nail-marks where he'd clawed the rowan off his skin.

'I didn't mean to hurt you,' she told him. 'With the bracelet, I was trying to help.'

Byron lowered his hands, watching the valley floor and the white dots of the sheep that grazed there. 'I didn't ask for your help,' he said. 'I don't want it.'

She moved closer, trying to stand in his line of sight. 'Why not? What's going on, Byron?'

'I don't need anyone's help. I'm not in trouble.'

'What about Gwenhidw?'

He smiled, remembering something. 'She wants to help too. She told me so.'

'She's a liar.'

'Don't say that. No, she isn't.'

Why was Byron defending her? 'She is a liar! You can't trust her.'

'Shut up, Cassie. You haven't got a clue what you're talking about.'

'Everyone keeps saying that! But it's not true. I know what I saw. She's a witch. She's cast some kind of awful spell and she's trying to take you away from us.' Her words flooded out, rushing over each other like water in a young stream.

Byron gave a cold laugh. 'She's not trying to take me away, Cassie. I'm trying to leave.'

# Chapter 14

Cassie was too stunned to speak. Byron *wanted* to leave.

'Why?' She felt like one of the rabbits that scurried over the mountain at dusk when a hawk swooped over. She was all thumping heart and frozen limbs.

'You don't know what it's like. To have Dad thinking you're a waste of space. To have him looking at you like that. You haven't got a clue, Cassie. He's not disappointed in you. I hear him sometimes, you know, when I'm up in my room and they're just below in the living room. The ceiling is thin as paper. I hear him wishing I'd chosen better subjects, wishing I'd done better in my mocks, wishing I was just a bit more like him.'

Cassie reached for him, wanted to touch his arm and tell him it was OK, but he thrashed his arm clear of her. He turned to face the valley and let the wind whip through his hair. 'It wasn't so bad when Taid was around. But now . . . It's just so lonely, Cassie.'

'But I'm right here,' she said.

'You're just a little kid.'

Somewhere, in the distance, she could hear the sound of

a plane, the bleat of one of the stupid sheep that must have wandered from its flock. She could hear the sound of her own pulse thumping in her throat.

Byron lurched away, heading back towards the footpath. 'We shouldn't even be here. You should be in school where you belong.'

'And where do you belong?' she yelled at his back.

He gave no reply. She was forced to break into a trot to catch up with him. 'What did she do to you?' Cassie demanded.

'Stop it,' he snapped. 'Stop messing in things you don't understand.'

If one more person said that to her, she was liable to punch them, hard. But there was no arguing, Byron had shut down and closed off in the way that drove everyone spare. Nagging would only make it worse.

The school was quiet when they reached it. The yard empty in the cold sunshine. Cassie was going to have to sign the late register and get buzzed into class. But she was too cross to care. Byron left without saying goodbye.

The school day passed in a blur. Cassie could hardly drag her attention to the project on the Romans that Mrs Khaleed was so excited about. So what if there used to be a Roman fort in Chester? Who cared if there was once a Roman villa in Wrexham? That was all a million years ago and nothing to do with the trouble Byron was in.

So, Cassie was glad to find Siân waiting for her after

school. She stood with the parents at the gates, all bundled up in her furry winter coat, with a pink and brown bobble hat balanced on her head.

'What's up with you?' Siân asked. 'You've a face like a wet Wednesday.'

Cassie hoiked her book bag up onto her shoulder and fell into step with her cousin as they walked towards home. 'I talked to Byron this morning. He prefers Gwenhidw to us.'

'He's an idiot.'

Cassie smiled despite herself. 'He *is* an idiot.'

'It's lucky for him that he's got us around.' Siân slipped her hand through the crook of Cassie's elbow and leaned into her. They turned onto the estate. Cassie stepped out of the way of a tired-looking woman with a pram and a toddler riding on the buggy board.

'He said he was lonely.'

'Oh, poor Byron,' Siân said.

'I know.'

They'd reached Cassie's road. She could see Tilda out in front of her house, lifting shopping from her Fiat 500. The fat ginger cat from three doors down was watching her do it. Cassie knew that if she made little *puss-puss-puss* noises at the cat it would trot close and wind itself around her ankles and purr like the car's engine. This was a friendly street – why couldn't Byron see that?

'Do you know what I did today?' Siân asked.

'No.'

'I read Taid's book, the one about the black ships.'

'What, all day?'

'Most of it, I am on holiday. It's good. It's about a war that goes on for ages and ages and to make it finally stop Odysseus tells his men to build a giant wooden horse. They all climb inside and then their enemy drags the horse into their city—'

'Why?'

'It's a bit of a plot hole, I agree. But they just do. And then Odysseus sneaks out of the horse at night and burns down the city.'

Cassie turned the handle on her front door and swung it open. 'I don't think I like Odysseus very much,' she said.

'That's Greek heroes for you,' Siân replied.

That evening, Byron wouldn't let Cassie anywhere near him to ask what Gwen might do. He kept his bedroom door shut tight and growled at Cassie and Siân whenever they went near. Worse was, Mam was defending him.

'Leave him be, girls. He's not well. He came home from school early. He doesn't need you two hanging off him like ivy.'

'We weren't—' Cassie tried.

But: 'I mean it. Stay away from his room. In fact, I'm sorry, Siân, but it might be better if you go back to Nain's for now, my love.'

So, Siân tramped back up the hill.

Mam decided she'd take Byron's tea up on a tray.

'What's up with the lad?' Dad asked as he watched her arrange a knife and fork around his nuggets, peas and chips.

'He's got a bit of a temperature,' Mam said. 'It will just be a cold.'

'He shouldn't have stayed out all night if he didn't want to get ill,' Dad said.

But Cassie couldn't help but feel frightened. What if this was Gwen's doing? Or worse, what if it was hers? She'd forced the rowan bracelet onto his wrist, even though he'd struggled. Had she hurt him?

She sat with Dad for the rest of the evening, watching a programme he'd chosen about explorers crossing Antarctica on a science channel. Normally, she'd moan about it until he changed it, but tonight, she was just glad to have him next to her, even if they didn't speak.

Byron woke her in the night. He woke them all. Yelling. Screaming. Thrashing in his bed as though wolves were chasing him across ice. Dad was the first one to run into Byron's room, in the T-shirt and boxers he slept in, not even pulling his slippers onto his feet.

Cassie saw from her own doorway.

In the darkness of the room, Dad leaned over Byron's bed. Cassie heard soft whispers.

The shrieking stopped, not abruptly, but as though Dad was slowly lowering the volume.

'You're all right, son,' Dad said. 'You're all right.'

Dad stood over the bed. He grasped both hands behind his back. He wasn't going to hug Byron, Cassie realised.

Hug him. *Hug him.*

Mam hovered on the landing. She flicked on the big light and Cassie was dazzled, momentarily, by the glare.

'Oh, everyone's up,' Dad said. 'It's like King's Cross Station.' He stepped out of Byron's room onto the landing.

'Is he sick?' Mam asked.

'Nightmare. You go into him.' Dad rubbed at his face. Somehow the sags and shadows were deeper than they were in daytime. 'This is all we need.'

Mam gave Cassie a quick, too-worried smile. 'You go back to sleep, cariad. There's nothing you can do.'

The infuriating thing, Cassie realised, was that that was true.

It didn't stop her wanting to do something though. Before she got ready for school, Cassie tried one last time to get Byron to tell her what was making him sick.

She crept into his room when Mam and Dad were downstairs, so she wouldn't be told off.

'What?' Byron groaned, from bed.

'How are you feeling?'

'Leave me alone.'

He had his duvet pulled right up to his face. His hair hung lank against his forehead. It was bound to give him spots.

She advanced on him, getting closer to the bed, until she

sat down heavily on the grey duvet. He smelled sour, like stale vinegar drying on chip wrappers.

He pulled the duvet higher and seemed to sink further into his pillows. She could just see an untidy mop of hair now.

'Byron . . .'

'I said leave me alone.'

'No!' She tugged at his duvet, trying to pull it off his face, they wrestled for a while, but, in the end, he was too weak, and she pulled it clear.

His skin really did look awful. Pale and patchy, as though it might slide off.

'You look like milk on the turn,' she said.

'Thanks.' He sighed heavily, the air coming right from the bottom of his lungs. 'I feel awful,' he admitted.

'What would make it better? Do you want to try Nain's bracelet?'

'Don't even think about it.' His hand went to his wrist, almost without thinking. He cupped the scratches, which were nearly healed.

'What, then?'

'The only thing I want is . . .' he trailed off.

'What?' she demanded.

He shook his head. Something awful occurred to Cassie. 'You want to go back there? Why, Byron? Why? What's so great about it?'

He closed his eyes. Paused. 'You didn't see what I saw. Feel what I felt.'

'What was it?'

'You can see things down there, things that you can't up here . . .'

'Like the beach? She showed us a beach. You can see one of those anytime, you just have to catch the bus to Barmouth.'

When he opened his eyes and looked at her again, they were filled with sadness. 'She showed me Dad. And Taid. I was there with them, down by the river in Tŷ Mawr, you know where it's shallow enough to go in, but deep enough to swim.'

Cassie knew exactly where he meant. It was just a little further along the valley floor, where the river made a lazy loop. She pressed her hand against the doorframe, holding herself up.

'Taid was splashing about in the water,' Byron said quietly. 'He'd taken his shoes off and left them on the bank. I ran right in when I saw him, in my trainers and everything. Taid and Dad laughed about it. You should've seen it, Cassie.'

'It was just a glimmer, Byron. That's what she called it. It wasn't real!'

'It felt real.'

Byron rolled over, pulled the duvet up close and buried himself down into it.

He was shutting her out completely.

# Chapter 15

The next morning, Byron was too ill for school. He looked pale and shivery. Mam wondered about the flu, maybe. She took two paracetamol and a glass of water into his room, then crept softly out, closing the door behind her. Cassie, who was drying her face in the bathroom, heard her feather-light sigh.

Mam met Dad at the bottom of the stairs. 'Perhaps I should give the surgery a ring?' she asked.

'For the flu? They won't be able to do anything.'

'I'll see if I can swap my shift so I can stay and keep an eye on him. Will you take Cassie out later?'

'Out?' Dad asked. 'Out where?'

Cassie's ears pricked up at the sound of her own name. She eased the bathroom door open a little more so she could hear better. She could see Dad looked cross and crumpled after a bad night's sleep, and none too happy about the idea of going anywhere.

'It's Bonfire Night,' Mam said. 'You should take her to the rugby club.'

Watching the bonfire and fireworks at the rugby club every year was a family tradition. They'd all go, wrapped up in coats and hats and scarves and watch the blossoms of fire against the night sky. It would be the first time Taid wouldn't be with them. And, it seemed, Mam and Byron would be missing too.

'Right,' Dad said, still not smiling. 'Right.'

Siân came with them. It was a chilly evening out and Cassie could see their breath rising in white clouds into the star-speckled sky. Even with the light from the streetlamps, the stars looked as though they'd been splashed on with a paintbrush. The cold made Cassie's ears tingle.

'Be careful!' Mam warned as they walked away from the house.

*Of what?*

Cassie jerked her hat down lower. The danger wasn't out here. Out here was all sparklers and candy floss. It was inside that the danger lurked. In Byron and whatever it was that he'd got himself into. Cassie shoved her hands into her pockets and felt the press of the bracelets against her side. She was wearing both rowan bracelets — hers and Byron's — the hardness of the wooden band made her feel stronger.

Byron was at home, with Mam watching over him. Mam wouldn't let Gwen take him. It just couldn't happen. Mam was a dragon when it came to her kids. Once, when Kieran in the year above had snipped at Cassie's ponytail with craft scissors, Mam had yelled blue murder at anyone who would listen. And Kieran had had to write a letter explaining why he was an idiot. Mam was fierce as anything.

Cassie slipped her hand through Dad's crooked elbow and hung off him as they walked, Siân on his other side. Mam would sooner fight the world than have anything bad happen to either of them. It was a very cheering thought. She gave a little skip and swung on Dad's arm.

'Whoa,' Dad laughed. 'You're full of beans.'

'I'm just excited, Dad. Aren't you?' She tugged down on his arm, feeling his muscles harden as he held her up.

'Excited, is it? I don't know. Fireworks aren't really my cup of tea. I never did get used to loud bangs where they shouldn't be.'

'It's OK, Dad,' she whispered. 'Fireworks can't hurt you.'

He laughed. The first belly-laugh she'd heard from him in a long time. Then he really flexed his arm, tucking her hand right in and reaching around to scoop her into a dancer's spin. The moon whirled above as Dad whisked her around. His face was wrinkled with smiles. Then he put her down.

Cassie leaned into Dad as they walked along past the empty school and the quiet main road. The rugby club was behind the old chapel. Its low clubhouse building had white walls and grey windows, and already they reflected back the peach and orange gleam of the bonfire.

The bonfire.

It was enormous. Piles of wood, pallets and offcuts, boards and skirting, with the odd kitchen chair and door, rose in a tottering pyramid in the middle of the car park, with a rope ring around it to keep people back. It was already burning. Dancing sparks floated upwards and winked out against the stars.

Cassie could feel the warmth pulsing from it, even though they were still only by the car park entrance. It was fully thirty paces away, but the flames belted out glorious heat.

The crowd were dark silhouettes between her and the bonfire. On the other side of the flames, faces were lit up with the amber glow, cheeks were pink, or warm gold, or bronze in the flamelight. There was Mrs Khaleed, with Mr Khaleed! Cassie waved frantically at her teacher, but she was so busy making sure that Mr Khaleed was filming the bonfire properly that she didn't notice. Gemma and Tilda, who lived on Cassie's street and had a dog called Smot, did spot her. Gemma had one hand resting protectively on her baby bump belly, the other, she raised and wiggled her fingers at Cassie.

Families and groups spread out right across the car park. Those further from the fire huddled inside green and brown and blue winter coats, like they'd wrapped parts of the mountains around themselves. Children ran about, carrying candyfloss and toffee apples wobbling on sticks. Others stood still, writing their names in light with sparklers. *Me, me, me,* over and over in glittering heat.

'Here,' Dad said. He dropped a few coins into both of their palms. 'For the sweets and what have you.'

'Can't we have a note?' Cassie asked.

Dad gave a reluctant grin. 'I'm not made of money. Stay out of trouble, I'm going to find a pint.'

She grabbed Siân's hand and pulled her closer to the fire.

Dad gave a tight wave, then plunged both hands into his pockets. The clubhouse door was ajar, and he headed towards the sound of the bar and the men gathered there.

Cassie was drawn to the blaze. The flames rolled in billowing sheets of red, gold and yellow. Dark shapes, burning furniture, crouched within the brightness. She could feel the skin on her cheeks tingle with the heat of it.

Siân pulled her hat off and tucked it into her coat pocket. 'It's roasting!' she said. 'Though my back is freezing.'

It was true, the freezing night was still crouched behind them, touching the backs of their necks and ankles with its icy fingers.

There was a small stall selling toffee apples in shiny wrappers. The stall-keeper twirled sticks in the circular steel pot and caught wisps of pink spun sugar. Cassie's mouth watered.

But, just then, the first fireworks shot up into the black, with a *pffft-crack*. Blue and red bursts, huge neon dandelion clocks filled the sky. Then, *peewww, peewww*, contra-trails of shimmering white and gold chased the dandelion clocks across the sky.

The small crowd cheered. In the distance, a clamour of rooks rose, protesting, into the dark.

The light, the heat, the crowd. It was magical. It was

enough to push all bad thoughts out of Cassie's mind. She felt herself twitching with glee.

'I wish Byron could see this,' she said.

'Maybe he can. Maybe he's watching from his bedroom window,' Siân replied. 'As long as he's got it locked, and doesn't let anyone in.'

'Who would he let in?' Cassie asked.

Just then Siân gripped her wrist, digging her fingers in too sharp, too tight.

'Hey!' Cassie complained.

Siân pointed at the bonfire. 'Look, Cassie. Look!' she urged.

It was hard, at first, to see what Siân was talking about. Looking at the flames left dancing green and blue shadows in the centre of her vision. Bodies in green and brown winter coats hung back, on the other side of the bonfire. It was a kaleidoscope movement of dark and light.

Then she saw.

One body, in a loose T-shirt that was way too cold for the season, despite the heat of the fire. The skin, poking out of the grimy fabric, glowed a yellow-green. Partly the reflection of the yellow bonfire, but partly, perhaps, the colour had seeped into him from the rocks and soils and roots he was usually surrounded by, a boy of moss and lichen.

Twm.

# Chapter 16

Twm danced as though he were alone on a desert island, not creeping at the edge of a crowd at the rugby club annual bonfire. His arms beetled around his head; the bangle on his wrist bounced. His hair tossed from side to side, long black locks that glinted in the flamelight. His body pulsed with a beat that was infectious, although the only music came from a small fairground ride, a little carousel where plastic donkeys and emus chased each other in a circle. He picked up an empty sweet wrapper and tucked it into the pocket of his shorts.

'Why is he here?' Siân wondered.

Cassie looked around to see if she could see Gwenhidw or any of the other tylwyth teg. But Twm appeared to be alone. None of the other people there, with their heads buried into hoods, thick scarves and candyfloss, paid him the slightest moment's attention.

'I don't care why he's here. But seeing as he is, he can tell us what's wrong with Byron.'

She moved through the crowd, weaving closer to the point on the other side of the fire where Twm danced in his own little world.

'Hey!' Cassie yelled, pushing through the crowd that were all looking up at the fireworks. 'Hey, Twm!'

A few people tutted as she barged through, a handbag swung too quickly and clouted her ear. People pressed away from her as she pushed through. Siân slipped behind in her wake.

Then, they were in front of him.

He danced on, smiling a contented little grin, his eyes closed, with his dark lashes resting on sunken circles under his eyes.

'Twm!' Cassie shouted right at him.

His eyes snapped open, and, for half a second, Cassie saw the telltale flash of blue magic before his pupils faded back to black. She had to remember that he wasn't a human boy, as much as he looked like one. He was one of the tylwyth teg.

'I know you,' he said, looking at Siân. He sounded surprised. 'I think we have met before? You're the one with the old stories. You gave me the names back, but I forgot them again. I dropped them down in the dark.'

'What names?' Cassie asked. 'What are you talking about?'

'And now you can see me. Humans aren't supposed to be able to see me.' He held his own hand up in front of his face, as if checking it was still there. His fingernails were as dirty as ever.

'Well,' Siân said, 'we can see you. You're standing right there.'

'Only the ones who've been invited in can see Annwn and the folk who live there,' Twm said, a little smugly.

'That's as maybe,' Siân said. 'But I can definitely see you.'

'We're looking right at you and we want to know, what's wrong with my brother?' Cassie planted her hands on her hips, and, despite the fluffy mittens, meant business. 'What's wrong with Byron?'

Twm raised his shoulders in a carefree shrug. 'How should I know? I've hardly even met him.'

'We want answers and you're going to give them to us,' Cassie told him.

Twm dropped his head to one side, considering her carefully. Then, without a word, he took a step back, away from the fire. Then another, and another. He was retreating into the darkness. Beyond the light from the fire, the black pitch was all shades and shadows. The twin posts at either end were wraith-white in the gloom. Past the far touchline stood a copse of bare trees, raising their straggle-branches to the sky.

'Where are you going?' Siân called after Twm.

Twm didn't look away, didn't stop walking.

Then, his body flickered — like bad phone reception — just flickered and was gone. Then, he was there again. On the pitch this time, near the goal. Flickered. Vanished. Then, *pop*, back again, this time with his legs hooked over the cross bar, body upside-down swinging in the air.

Cassie gasped. She couldn't help it. It felt as if her body had been winded. To see such, well, *magic*. It was — incredible, impossible. Twm had shifted like the Cheshire

111

cat in the Disney film. One minute there, the next, somewhere else entirely and enjoying himself while he was at it.

Cassie felt so out of her depth she might as well be drowning.

Her fingers clamped around Nain's bracelet, a reassurance that they weren't alone in all this.

'After him,' Siân yelled. She broke into a run. The turf was soft underfoot. The grass mown short, ready for the shove and surge of the game.

It was absolutely forbidden to go onto the pitch — no dog-walking, or after school kickabouts. It was just for matches. Men from the village grunting over a ball. Sometimes women too. But not kids. Not Cassie. She had never, ever run on this grass before. Never dared, for fear of getting the worst telling off of her life.

But now, she had to. There was no choice. Twm, in all likelihood, knew what was wrong with Byron, and might even know how to fix it.

There was no question that Cassie was going to keep to the rules. She ran onto the pitch towards the goal, as fast as if she had a rugby ball tucked under her arm and an easy try in sight.

Siân was right on her shoulder.

Twm swung happily, back and forth, upside-down from the crossbar, hair trailing, arms hanging loose towards the ground. He was a pennant hanging from a castle keep, a flag in the breeze.

She was breathless by the time they reached him. Not only from running. Just looking at his smile, upside down, with canine teeth pointing up, was enough to make her heart race.

'You again?' he drawled.

'You tell us what we want to know,' Cassie insisted.

Twm gave away nothing but that infuriating smile. So like Byron when he was being annoying.

'What's wrong with my brother? Why is he so sweaty and pale and tired? And why are his eyes sometimes blue?'

Twm trailed his fingers through the air as though he were playing invisible harp strings. 'There's nothing at all the matter with him. He'll be fit as a fiddle when he comes home.'

'He *is* home!'

'If you say so.'

Cassie had the strong urge to punch Twm. But then, she had a better idea. She pulled back her sleeve, held up her wrists and the bracelets that hung from them.

Twm flinched as though she might scald him.

He flickered: there-gone-there-gone-there—

Cassie grabbed at his dangling wrists and held on tight. *Please let the rowan block his magic.* Tremors ran across his skin. She could see glowing pulses of blue magic straining in his forearms, but the bracelets she wore kept him bound – for now.

'What did Gwenhidw do to Byron?' Cassie demanded.

Twm snapped and snarled at her, angry as a cat. She could feel his skin writhing; bands of muscle and sinew taut and twisting under her fingertips. Holding his wrists was like holding a leather sock full of worms.

It was gross.

She wanted to let go. Drop her hands and wipe them on the back of her jeans.

But she held on.

'Stop wriggling!' Cassie insisted.

'Stop!' Siân snapped, sounding a lot like Mrs Khaleed.

Twm stopped. His body stilled, though his eyes followed them hungrily.

'It's best not to show fear,' Siân told Cassie. 'I saw it on a programme about the wolves in Scotland.'

'But you should be scared,' Twm whispered. The threat was all the worse for being quiet. Cassie felt it settle inside her like ice drunk too quickly.

'Why?' Cassie asked. 'Why should we be scared?'

'Because Gwenhidw has noticed you. She knows your names. That never ends well for humans.' He shifted desperately, uncomfortable under her grip. But Cassie kept her fingers squeezed tight. She tried to swallow down the repulsion she felt.

'Why is she interested in us?' Siân asked.

'She's not interested in you,' Twm spat.

'You just said—'

'She's interested in your brother, and you have somehow

managed to put yourself in the way of her looking. You were foolish enough to step into her gaze. She didn't come looking for you.'

'Why is she interested in Byron? He's an idiot.' Cassie couldn't help herself.

Twm laughed. It sounded loud out here at the edge of the pitch, but no one over by the bonfire so much as glanced in their direction.

Under her fingers, the writhing was slowing down, beginning to feel more like a boy than a beast. Was the power of the bracelet fading? Cassie sensed that he might vanish any moment. 'Tell me what I want to know.'

'He asked for an invitation, he joined the dance at the door of Annwn. All Gwen did was open the door, let him in. He's Helynt now. He's family. And he's pining because he's away from his family.'

Cassie's eyes prickled with tears. 'He's *with* his family. He's with Mam right now.'

'Some of him is. But he gave part of himself to Gwen. And he won't rest until he's whole again. He gave her a gift. It was foolish of him to give her a gift.'

'What gift?' Cassie demanded. 'What did he give her?'

Twm hissed at her, darting his face towards hers. She was forced back, in fright. With that, Twm wrenched his wrists free of Cassie's grip and faded, faded, faded until he was gone.

# Chapter 17

'What in the name of all that's holy are you two doing? Get off that pitch, right now!' A very angry, very loud voice shouted at them from the direction of the car park.

Cassie stepped under the white crossbar of the goal – Twm had disappeared completely so the way was clear – and over the dead-ball line on the other side. Siân was right beside her. They were off the pitch.

'And stay off!' the angry voice added, 'Or I'll be having words with your mam and dad.' The shouting shape stepped back into the dark mass of the crowd around the bonfire. The leaping yellow flames were burning down into red, throbbing embers.

'I want to find Dad,' Cassie said. Her insides were a washing-machine whirl of feelings. Byron was homesick, Twm had said. Homesick for the cave under the mountain, with its strange cavern full of rubbish and its half-dead blackthorn tree. How could he want that, and not the neat, cosy house with them and the village cwtshed around it?

How could Byron not want Cassie?

'I think Uncle Gareth's in the clubhouse,' Siân said, slipping her arm around Cassie's shoulders, pulling her into a hug.

Cassie wrapped her own arms about herself, trying to hold her seams together. She might unravel like torn wool. The distant bonfire was a beacon, pulling her closer to its light and warmth.

They walked through the chattering, laughing crowd to the clubhouse.

The door to the bar was propped open, despite the cold weather. Beyond the porch, a second inner door, covered in flapping signs saying things like *No boots beyond this point* and *No children after 8pm*, kept out the worst of the night air. Cassie could hear the rumble of adult conversations, the mixed smell of wet dog, drying coats and bitter spills that was kind of gross, but also kind of not.

Cassie pushed against the door of the bar and went in to find Dad. There was the sound of cheerful chatter, conversation jumped between tables as one group butted in with an opinion, or comment, or quick joke. All the tables were full and there were people standing at the bar.

She looked around. Where was he?

There.

Right in the far corner, away from the windows and the view of the bonfire. Dad sat on a low stool, alone. His fingertips rested on a nearly-finished beer, the froth had made white tide marks on the inside of the glass. A second pint, full to the brim with caramel coloured liquid, sat untouched on the dented copper tabletop. Dad had placed the full pint in front of an empty bar stool.

Cassie and Siân approached.

Dad gave a little start, as though she'd roused him from sleeping.

'Hello, trouble,' Dad said.

'Hi, Daddy,' Cassie replied.

Dad's eyes searched her face. He looked worried, concerned. No, that wasn't quite it. He looked sad, she realised, his forehead pinched miserably.

'It's odd, isn't it,' Dad said, 'the way time just carries on regardless? First Bonfire Night without Taid.' He gestured to the untouched beer and the empty stool beside his. 'Another first.' He sighed.

Cassie had no idea what to say. She'd wanted Dad to pull her into a hug and tell her it was all going to be OK, that Byron would be safe and sound and nothing was ever going to hurt him. But here Dad was, hurting in his own way.

Dad tipped up his own glass and downed the last inch of liquid. He wiped his mouth with the back of his hand. 'Well. I suppose it's time to head back. Are you girls ready?'

Cassie nodded. 'I think so.'

'Good. Let's go.'

They left the clubhouse, and the car park with the stars twinkling cold and distant above them.

# Chapter 18

The next day, there was absolutely no way on earth that Cassie could settle to anything. Byron was homesick for a hole in the ground. Gwen was pulling him in with her horrible magic. Dad was sad and sorry and hadn't a clue what was really going on. It was down to her and Siân. And she, for one, was sick of waiting and seeing, she wanted to *do* something.

So, she was thrilled to see Siân and Nain waiting for her at the school gate when the bell went. The yard was a blur of charging Year Threes and squealing Year Fours. Miss Saunders, wearing the high-vis vest that meant she was in charge of home time, yelled at some Year Five boys to stay inside the gates. There was Nain, all done up for a day out, waving madly.

'I told Nain about seeing Twm again,' Siân said. 'I looked online to see if Twm was there, or Gwenhidw, but there was next to nothing. How can there be a monster under a mountain and she doesn't even have a Wikipedia page?'

Cassie shrugged.

Nain dropped a quick kiss on the top of her head. 'So, I suggest we go to the library. They have a whole section on local history.'

'The library?' Cassie asked.

'The library,' Siân said firmly.

'I was thinking more that we raid Annwn under cover of darkness and advance on Gwen with all guns blazing,' Cassie said.

'All what blazing?' Nain asked sharply.

'Not *real* guns, Nain. It was just a, a whatchamacallit?'

'A metaphor?' Siân suggested.

Cassie nodded.

'We can't fight Gwen with a metaphor,' Siân said.

That was true. But they needed all *something* blazing if they were going to get Byron back. And for that they would need to know Gwen's weaknesses.

'OK, the library,' Cassie agreed.

The village library was at the edge of the estate, built when the first hopeful streets popped up. It was a small building, much smaller than the school, a single storey block with pale lemon walls and a green door. Cassie had visited a lot when she was younger and Mam had time to join in with songs about wheels on buses. It had been a while though, since she'd pushed open the heavy brass handle and stepped inside.

Nain, on the other hand, was here all the time; she came to swap her crime novels and complained whenever the council threatened to cut its opening hours. She waved them in as though it was her own front room. Siân's glasses steamed up in the warmth of the interior; she took them off and wiped them with her thumb.

'Ooh, Sandra, su'mae?' the lady behind the desk greeted Nain. 'We've got the new Ian Rankin in. I've put it aside for you.'

'That's great, Nessa, thank you. But I'm here with my granddaughters today.'

The lady smiled at Cassie and Siân. 'Oh lovely. You know where the children's section is, Sandra. Let me know if you need any help.'

Siân ignored the children's section with its battered boxes of picture books and bright carpets and cushions. Instead, she scanned the shelves and stopped at a section labelled *Local history*. She put her bag down on a nearby table and turned to face the books, all business.

There were lots of hardback books on sensible subjects. A few were displayed with their covers out. Cassie saw pictures of miners and collieries, men in hard hats with faces black with coal dust, or pictures of castles with banners waving from the battlements.

'*Pits and Princes*,' Nain said. 'That's Wales, all right.' She reached for a book the size of a small breezeblock and opened it to reveal tiny, tiny print. '*Wales in the Middle Ages*?' she read. 'It will be *Wales in Old Age* by the time I get through this.' She slipped it back in place on the shelf.

Siân, who was busy unpacking supplies – three pens, a notebook, her own copy of *Welsh Fairy Tales, Myths and Legends*, with page corners folded in dog-ears – looked over. 'We've got to be systematic,' she said. 'We can't just read everything here in the hope we find something useful. The library closes at six.'

Cassie and Nain shared a relieved look.

'Here's what we know,' Siân opened her notebook and looked at some notes. 'Years ago, the tylwyth teg enticed a boy called Alun Wyn Roberts into Annwn. He was able to tell people about it, but days later he disappeared, never to be seen again. Missing, presumed dead. The pattern is repeating with Byron. Twm told us that Byron was foolish enough — Twm's words, not mine,' Siân clarified, before Nain could tell her off for calling her cousin a fool. 'Byron was foolish and gave Gwen a gift and that's her hold over him.'

Cassie nodded, and picked up a biro of her own. Siân made a pretty good researcher, as it turned out.

'What we don't know,' Siân explained, 'is why Gwen took Alun Wyn, what she intends to do with Byron. We also don't know what sort of gift he might have given her. Nain, you look through the indexes of any books there on myths, legends, the tylwyth teg, look for gifts given to them, spells, enchantments, that sort of thing. Look out for any mention of the derew too, the strange beasts we saw in Annwn.'

'I'm going to look for more information about Gwenhidw herself,' Siân said, as she flipped to a blank page in her notebook. 'Who is she? What does she want? There's got to be answers here.' She gestured at the shelf full of books.

That was a lot of reading.

A lot of reading.

Cassie wiggled her toes in her trainers. 'What about me? I want to help, but you're a faster reader than I am.'

Nain looked up from the table she'd settled on, pen in hand, 'Practice makes perfect,' she muttered.

'Could you research Alun Wyn?' Siân suggested. 'He wouldn't be in the books, I don't think, but there might be more about him on the library computers or the local newspaper archives?' She pointed at the library's three chunky computers. The council's logo tracked across their dark screens. 'There will be news stories.'

'On it,' Cassie said.

They had a plan: Nain was hunting spells, Siân was hunting history and Cassie was to find out exactly what had happened to Gwen's last victim. It felt already as though Byron was one step closer to being safe.

Cassie clicked on the local newspaper app and typed keywords into the search bar: *Alun Wyn Roberts.*

It didn't take long before all kinds of old items popped up. It was surprising how many people had had Alun or Wyn or Roberts in their names: someone who'd once attempted a world record bagpipe performance called Alun Jones Roberts; a farmer called Gareth Alun Wyn who'd got into a planning dispute with a neighbour. She added quotation marks and *Penyfro* to her search. There! *Local Boy Missing.*

There was a photo of a smiling teenage boy, captioned *Alun Wyn Roberts*. A school photo, with a mottled brown background. Cassie could imagine a queue of children, waiting to file in front of the camera, smoothing down their clothes, rubbing sleep from their eyes. Had Taid been there when this was taken? Waiting in the queue? Perhaps watching as this boy settled on the stool and was told to 'say cheese'?

She read the article. One day in November, fifty years ago, almost to the day, Alun Wyn hadn't come home from secondary school. The bus had rattled from town, to the village, dropping off children along its route. Alun Wyn had got off, as usual, in Penyfro, but he hadn't stepped through his front door. No one knew where he had gone. His mother told the police that he had been poorly a few days earlier, but he'd seemed well enough to go to school. No one had seen him again.

Cassie sat, very still, looking at the boy on the screen.

She checked the date today – 6th November. She checked the date on the news item – 9th November. Three days away. Was it a coincidence? Nain had said that Alun Wyn bragged about meeting the tylwyth teg. He'd been laughed at for it. Then, a few days later, he disappeared.

Would it be Mam soon, making statements to the police, answering reporters' questions?

Not if Cassie could help it.

She hit print on the story and took the copy to the table

where Nain and Siân pored over their stack of books. Both of their notebooks were filling up, Cassie noticed. Good. She took a seat beside them. The library hummed with the sound of after-school families: chatter at the desk about the weather and the roadworks; little kids flapping picture books, demanding 'Again, again'; the cough and paper rustle as someone settled in to read the day's news. It all sounded so normal. So *Penyfro.*

Yet there was a monster lurking deep in the mountain, and that monster was coming for Byron.

'What have you found?' she asked. 'Anything?'

Siân pushed her glasses up her nose and looked up. 'There are a few references to Gwen scattered about.'

Cassie peered over Siân's elbow to see the book she had open. The text was tiny and packed onto the page. There wasn't a single picture, which seemed a shame in a book about magic.

'I found Alun Wyn,' Cassie told them. She laid the picture down on the table.

The library printer was black and white, but it was still clear enough to make Nain gasp. 'Oh, yes. That's him,' she said, sadly. 'He was such a nice boy.'

Cassie, wanting to distract Nain from more sadness, asked Siân, 'What did you find about Gwen?'

'Bits and pieces. Nobody knows much. She's in a few different legends. Some of them are really old. Ancient. Some say she might have been in Wales from the time of King Arthur. She might even have known him.'

'If you'd met King Arthur, what could you possibly want with Byron?' Cassie wondered.

'It's all a bit tangled up.' Siân ran her fingertip along the blocky paragraphs. 'But King Arthur in real life probably wasn't the fancypants king with the round table. He was probably a Roman general who defended the island against the Anglo-Saxons. If he existed.'

'Well, Gwen exists, I don't see why King Arthur wouldn't.'

Siân continued scanning the page. 'She might be even older than him, though. She's almost part of nature, clouds and water and trees. In one story, she's a lake.'

It wasn't clear at all to Cassie how someone might be a lake. Would they still have a face? What would they eat?

Nain sighed. 'Who'd have thought it possible? For nearly two thousand years she's been here, if those tales are true.'

'What did you find, Nain?' Siân asked.

Nain picked up her notebook and flicked through a few pages. 'There's nothing in here about derew, not a word. But there's quite a lot here about the tylwyth teg and magic. They're mischievous. They can be good or bad, depending on their mood. The blackthorn tree is also full of magic; it's said to guard the underworld, so it's associated with death. But it's like the tylwyth teg, it's got its good side too. From what I can tell, the tylwyth teg are more like imps, they make trouble without even trying.'

Cassie folded her arms. 'Gwen doesn't seem like an imp. She's scary as anything.'

'Imps can be scary,' Nain said, 'if you get on the wrong side of them.' Nain pulled the book she'd been reading closer and traced the tip of her biro down a page. 'Oh dear. Oh dear.'

'What?'

'What is it?'

'This says you should never, ever give anything you own to spell-weavers. It gives them power over you. It says even giving them a hair from your head is enough.'

'What's a spell-weaver? Is Gwen one?' Siân asked, trying to read over Nain's shoulder.

'I think the author of this book is using fancy words,' Nain said. 'I think it means witches and fairies and the like.'

Cassie wasn't bothered by what Gwen was *called*, she was much more worried about what she could *do*. 'So, Byron could have given Gwen anything? Absolutely anything?' It wasn't even necessarily something decent like a skateboard, or his PlayStation, even though that was old now. If it could be *anything* then they might never work it out in time to save him.

The three sat in silence for a moment, taking it all in. They were looking for a needle in a haystack and they didn't even know what the needle looked like.

# Chapter 19

'I need to ask an expert,' Nain told them. The library was closing and, though they had scanned out as many books as Nain's library card would let them, she was worried they wouldn't say more about what Byron might have given Gwen or what she would do with his gift. 'I've got a friend who works at the county museum. Let me speak to her about all this.'

'Who do *you* know who'd work at a museum?' Siân asked as she tested the weight of her backpack.

'Hey, cheeky,' Nain said. 'Not everyone born in Penyfro left school at sixteen, you know. Some people even went to university! And my friend Carys was one of them. In the meantime, you girls stay away from the railway track, do you hear?'

Cassie said nothing. She helped carry the mini-library back to Nain's house. But, once she had done that, she was a girl with a very definite, decided mission.

'I have to force him,' Cassie told Siân. 'I have to make Byron tell me what he gave to Gwen and then we have to get it back.'

'Will he tell you?' Siân asked doubtfully.

It was true that Byron had reacted very badly to her offers of help so far. But he couldn't really want to be spirited away from home — could he? Things weren't that bad for him, surely?

Mind you, she couldn't remember the last time they had all four done anything together without it ending in shouting and slammed doors. Dad was on edge all the time. Mam was so tired. And Byron was a whirlwind of sad and angry and stupid.

'I'll *make* him,' Cassie said.

She walked back to the estate through the damp early evening. All the flurry and fuss of Bonfire Night was gone and now it just felt like autumn was turning everything to wet mush. 'I'll *make* him,' she told the parked cars and the low walls and Mrs-Owens-across-the-way's bird table.

She stepped into the house, still steeled to force Byron to speak. She kicked her shoes off. He was on the couch, in the living room. He was cocooned in his duvet, a fat, grey grub. What would he be when Gwen was done with him? Squished like a bug? There was a bowl of crisps beside him, uneaten, and he held the remote control, flicking, flicking, flicking through channels, not even pausing to see if the show was a good one.

'Byron!'

He grunted from under the duvet.

'Tell me what you gave Gwen!' she prodded him hard. 'Tell me.'

In a furious flurry of movement, the duvet shot back and Byron reared up — like a vampire surging from a coffin. His face was pale as winter, his hair lank. But his eyes, *his eyes* blazed blue, lit from within.

He leaped to his feet. The remote clattered to the floor and the volume on the telly jumped right up: *Add the beaten eggs slowly, folding them into the mixture without losing the fluffy consistency.*

'Leave. Me. Be.' He yelled, right in her face, leaning down at her so that she was made to notice just how much bigger he was than her. How wide his shoulders. How strong he was. Cassie staggered back and caught her calf muscle on the edge of the coffee table.

'Ow!' she felt tears burn her eyes.

'Serves you right,' Byron said. He stalked from the room, fury making his spine rigid.

Cassie heard him run up the stairs, taking them two by two.

'For God's sake,' Dad yelled from the kitchen. 'Byron, will you turn that ruddy racket down?'

Cassie picked up the remote control and switched off the TV.

# Chapter 20

'It's OK. It will be OK,' Siân soothed Cassie. She'd come round first thing and found Cassie still upset about the Byron she'd seen the night before. She was curled up in her own bed, bedroom door firmly closed. Siân kneeled on the rug, stroking Cassie's hair.

'Have you talked to your mam?' Siân asked.

Cassie nodded into her pillow. 'A little bit last night.' Her mouth tasted fuzzy, her hair stuck limply to her cheek. 'Mam says I'm not to bother him. That he's a raging ball of hormones and more crotchety than usual and I'm just to give him a wide berth. For my sake and his, she says.' Mam couldn't see what was right under her nose, she couldn't see past the adolescent hormones and teenage strops. She couldn't see what was so plain to Cassie — they were losing Byron.

'Look,' Siân said. 'Come on. Sit up. Let me get—'

She stood and left the room. Cassie heard a tap running. Moments later, Siân was back with a damp flannel. 'Wipe your face, it will make you feel better.'

The rough, cool cloth was a balm. Cassie managed to sit up.

'I think I have an idea,' Siân said. 'I was thinking some

more about the gift, and it made me think of some of the stories in *Welsh Fairy Stories*.'

'And?'

'Well. There are lots of legends about the tylwyth teg and humans. And a lot of them are about food.'

'Food?' Cassie moved the cloth to her neck, feeling a bit more herself.

'They seem a bit obsessed with it. I mean, it stands to reason. Who knows what they get to eat down there in the dark? In one story, a girl forgets to give them milk so they swap her baby brother for one of the tylwyth teg. In another, a prince gets them to forgive some insult by throwing a big feast.'

'You want to throw a feast?'

Siân shook her head. 'No. Not exactly. What if we find Twm, and take him some nice food, as a gift? And, in return, we ask him to tell us what Byron gave to Gwen that has him trapped?'

Cassie pushed back her duvet cover. 'Like a bribe, you mean?'

That could work. Twm had been good to them, and shown them the way to the Fiedown, when Siân had reminded him of the stories he'd lost.

'But we absolutely shouldn't give Twm a gift of something that belongs to us,' Cassie warned. 'You heard what Nain said about that. We can't let him have power over us.'

'I'm going to take the food out of your fridge,' Siân said. 'It doesn't belong to me. I'll give that to him. It's a loophole.'

Cassie rubbed her face, clearing sleep. It seemed like Siân had thought it all through. 'But where will we find Twm? He won't still be at the rugby club?'

Siân glanced down. 'No. We'll have to go to Annwn.'

'Siân! Nain said we weren't to go there again.' Cassie was up and out of bed. She pulled on a jumper — it didn't seem right to argue with Siân while still in her Hello Kitty pyjamas.

'I know, but what choice do we have? Her museum friend won't be able to tell us what Byron gave Gwen, will she? And he's made it clear that he won't tell us. We have to risk it.'

Did they? Cassie hated disobeying Nain. But Byron had looked so awful last night, so angry and . . . frightening.

She was frightened of her own brother, she realised. It was an awful, awful feeling, it felt like a hole in the middle of her chest letting all the air out of her lungs.

'OK,' she said. 'I'm in. Let's do it.' She pulled on a pair of black leggings and some socks. She pulled a brush through her hair a few times. Doing such ordinary things helped to slow her pulse a little. It would be all right, she told herself. Siân's plan would work. They'd give Twm a treat and he'd tell them what they needed to know.

She had a sudden thought. 'We should take him that book too!' Cassie suggested. 'That one of Taid's with the story about the wooden horse and that man with the funny name.'

'Odysseus. Yes, I think Twm would really like that. Maybe we should tell Nain after all, we should ask if it's all right to take the book.'

133

Cassie shook her head firmly. 'No, you were right before. It's best Nain doesn't know. She'd give us the book if we ask, but if we ask, she'd stop us going. Better not to ask.'

'OK. I'll get the food from here,' Siân said, 'then, I'll run and get the book, and then—'

'We go back into Annwn,' Cassie said.

The tunnel mouth yawned black against the pale blue sky. Skeleton trees reached dark fingers towards the wispy clouds. There was no sound coming from the tunnel, except the occasional *ploop* as water dripped from the ceiling into puddles. Cassie shone a torch beam onto the dark bricks, they glistened back at her as though giant slugs had slithered over them.

Cassie held a carrier bag full of the nicest things Siân could find in their cupboards: chocolate buttons; a box of fake Jaffa Cakes, which Mam said were just as good as the real thing; some mini Mars bars and a carton of apple juice with its own straw stuck to the side. And Taid's copy of *Black Ships Before Troy.*

Together they walked in. The air was thick with the smell of caves, damp and cold. The crunch of their footsteps echoed.

The torch threw a small puddle of light for them to step into, with darkness pressing at their back and sides. As the mouth swallowed them up, Cassie felt that the air was different. It wasn't damp and clammy like last time they'd been here. It felt more electric; the hairs on her head seemed to tingle with it. The torchlight bounced back in just the same way, but the echo of their footsteps came from further away, as though they were walking in a chasm, not a tunnel.

Then, she felt the earth beneath her feet start to slope gently downwards.

The door to Annwn was open.

# Chapter 21

Cassie and Siân followed the railway tunnel down. The walls changed from black brick to the softer, squishier red-brown, shot through with blue light. They walked past the spot where they had first met Twm, through the opening into the wide central corridor.

Cassie clutched the carrier bag of treats, squeezing the handles tight. The corridor was empty. High, high above them the blue veins of light interlaced like streams of rain flowing over glass. The dark doorways that led who-knows-where in the warren were eyeless sockets looking back at her. The scrawls of black shapes, people, animals, houses, plants, were a dark riot on the walls.

Where would Twm be?

They couldn't just wander down here aimlessly. It was huge.

As if Siân had read Cassie's mind, she said, 'We should go down towards Fiedown, where the tylwyth teg sleep.'

'What if Gwen's there?' Cassie twisted the bag, letting the plastic dig into her wrist.

'Then we make sure she doesn't see us.'

Before they headed off, Cassie checked to see that the drawing of Penyfro Mountain was still beside their entrance way. It was. She touched her fingertips to it gratefully.

Then, they headed on. They could hear their own footsteps, no matter how softly they tried to walk. Cassie wished she could quiet the thumping of her heart.

'What was that?' Siân stopped. Looked up. They both listened. Was it a faint cry? Had someone called out? Or was the darkness playing tricks on them? Cassie held Siân's frightened stare, the whites of her eyes clear to see. The shout, if there had been one, didn't come again. They kept walking.

*Hie!*

The cry was closer this time. Accompanied by footsteps. Someone, something, running towards them? Or away? The echo made it impossible to locate.

'Down!' Siân whispered. They both dropped to the ground, as far into the shadow of the wall as they could. Cassie had found a dark hoodie to go with her leggings. Hopefully they were like two small stones, barely there in the blackness.

She risked a peek. Two tylwyth teg, neither of them Twm, ran from one of the openings, glanced about quickly then plunged into a different side passage. The lead boy yelled again at the girl who ran behind.

They hadn't spotted Cassie and Siân, curled up small.

'This might not be such a good idea,' Cassie said.

'It's the best one we've got.' Siân helped her to her feet.

They kept to the wall, ready to drop and curl up like woodlice if the tylwyth teg came back. Perhaps it was their ears getting more attuned to the sounds, or perhaps it was fear raising phantoms, but it seemed that there were sounds of life coming from all directions now — distant shouts, stones kicked by scurrying feet, even, once, the certain sound of breathing coming from somewhere way too close for comfort.

Cassie forced her feet to keep moving. For Byron, for Mam and Dad, she had to do this.

They reached the main crossroads. The place where the sides of the corridor gave way to two enormous arches; on one side, the Tanglement, with its strange piles of objects, a museum to the world above; on the other the Thorn Hall. It was the hall that drew Cassie. In the blue light the bare branches of the enormous, gnarled tree threw prying finger-shadows on the ground. The air smelled dry and dusty, though the skeletal leaves strewn about suggested it might once have been lush with growth.

Cassie entered the hall.

'Where are you going?' Siân asked.

'I just want a quick look.'

'But what about—'

'I'll be quick.' She wanted to touch the tree. Although it looked old, and ill, tired under the weight of itself, there was something gentle about it. Like an old dog who just wanted to lie out on a sunny porch, or a grandparent settling down in a comfy armchair. She could almost hear its sigh. Nain's nain thought blackthorn trees were used in evil spells by witches. But the book in the library had said that they were a mixture of good and evil — the way most people were, she supposed. It felt like a person, somehow, a tired person who'd seen and done enough.

Cassie stepped under the branches, right up to the enormous trunk. The bark was patterned with deep ridges, years and years of growth. She rested her palms flat, and, for a moment, Annwn wasn't quite so scary, it might be the home of a monster, but it wasn't only monsters here.

'You cannot keep following me everywhere I go.' The voice came from above. She looked up. There was Twm, curled up in the crook of one of the lower branches, looking as cool as anything.

'We found you!' Cassie said, delighted.

'You shouldn't be looking,' Twm snapped. He lowered himself down, hanging from the branch with both hands before dropping, with bent knees, to the floor.

'We've brought you something,' Siân said, 'but it's not a gift. And it never belonged to us.'

'It's a bribe,' Cassie added.

'A trade,' Siân corrected.

'What trade?' Twm was interested, it was clear. His head tipped to one side and the crotchety look of a few moments before was gone.

Siân took the carrier bag from Cassie and held it out, handles spread open, revealing the feast inside.

Twm dropped his head to look, gave an excited growl, and reached for the box of fake Jaffa Cakes.

Cassie reached out to cover the bag with her palm. 'Not so fast. It's a trade, which means you have to give us something. Siân, tell him.'

Twm's eyes narrowed as he glared at the bag and the rowan bracelet on her wrist, Cassie saw the unmistakable flash of blue as a current of magic shot through him.

'I've been reading all about you,' Siân said. 'In all the legends you lot seem to really like treats. Cakes and fresh milk and sweet porridge, stuff like that?'

Twm gave a shrug that might have been yes and might have been no.

'We'll give you everything in the bag if you can tell us what Byron gave to Gwen and how we can get it back.'

Twm barked a short laugh. 'I can't tell you that.'

'How about if I add this?' Siân put the carrier bag down and swung her backpack around. She pulled out Taid's book and held it so he could see the cover: the prow of a ship cutting through waves, a golden eye painted on the wood, glaring at its destination. 'It's all about the Trojan War.'

His fingers reached out for the book, his face, for a moment, didn't look like the face of a half-wild tylwyth teg, it was the face of a curious little boy. Then he snatched his fingers back. 'What use is that to me? I can't read it.'

Siân opened the cover, 'It's illustrated.'

Twm's eyes widened as he saw the gods, the monsters, the heroes within. It was clear that he was hungry for the book, that he yearned for it more than for all the chocolate treats squished together. For the first time, Cassie wondered what the stories meant to him. Why was he so interested, when he had magic of his own, and the glimmers and wonders that Gwen could conjure?

'Give it to me,' Twm said.

'Tell us what Byron gave first,' Siân replied.

Twm squirmed on the spot. Then he threw up his hands. 'Zounds! I can't tell you because I don't know, all right? I can't remember. I can't even remember if I ever knew. I forget so much, all the time.' Twm's face furrowed into a deep sadness, a sadness that was at once of the moment and at the same time long, long held. Twm's sadness sat close to the surface. He shook his head. 'I can't tell you, none of the Helynt can.'

So, there it was. If the only people who knew were Gwen and Byron, and neither of them were telling, then there was no hope. Cassie felt as sad as Twm looked.

'Well,' Siân said suddenly, 'what *can* you tell us?'

'What do you mean?'

'I don't know. Why does she even want Byron? What's she going to do with him? Will he be turned into a boar and hunted by his own dogs? Not that he has any dogs. But that's the sort of thing you do, isn't it? What did she do with Alun

Wyn? Did he die? How did he die? Do you know any of that?'

Siân lifted the carrier bag and swung it gently by the handles. Was Twm tempted?

'I'll tell you what I know,' he said. He snatched the bag in a flash, and the book too. He hugged them close for a second, his eyes closed as the hard cover pressed against his chest. Then, he was all business. 'Sit,' he said.

Cassie dropped to the floor. The soft ground had been made by leaves upon leaves upon leaves slowly falling and flaking. Under the arching branches, on the comfortable earth, Cassie almost forgot, for a moment, that they were in danger. Twm opened the book reverently. His fingers traced the words, but it was the illustrations that had him rapt, from the green-haired sorceress with the golden apple on the first page, to the wooden horse and fall of the city at the end, he was enchanted. Siân tore open the Jaffa Cakes and ate one before passing them to Twm.

As he bit, and chewed the orangey jammy chocolate, he looked at the pages open on his lap.

'So,' Siân prompted. 'What can you tell us? What does Gwen want with Byron?'

# Chapter 22

'Gwenhidw wants your brother because Annwn is in trouble,' Twm said. 'Look!' He pointed up at the colossal tree above them. 'See how sick it is. It hasn't blossomed for so long we can hardly remember the smell of its flowers. The leaves it has are curling and dying.'

The tree had reminded Cassie of something old, something in the last days of its life. She rested her hand on its trunk companionably. 'What's that got to do with Byron, though?'

'I'm getting to that.' Twm took another bite of cake and chewed it slowly before eventually swallowing it. 'It's not just the blackthorn that's weakening, the derew are too.'

'What *are* derew?' Siân asked.

'You two are very impatient,' Twm scolded. 'I won't tell you anything if you keep interrupting.'

'Sorry.'

Twm nodded. 'Gwen is the Guardian of the derew. We help her, but she keeps them safe. Once upon a time they were tree spirits, they could grow as big as an oak. But they're getting smaller, weaker like the blackthorn. They might die. If they keep getting weaker, they will die and all the woods of the world will wither.'

Cassie thought back to the strange creatures she'd seen in Fiedown, the greeny-brown creatures that looked like beetles but behaved like sheep. Were they really tree spirits?

Twm's explanation was giving her more questions than answers.

He ignored her squirming and pulled the chocolate buttons from the bag. He tore open the packet and let one melt on his tongue. 'Your brother will fix them, for a while at least. His future, the years he would have had up there, where you come from, Gwen will give those years to the blackthorn and the derew. They will recover, for a while.'

'What?' Cassie yelped. Twm was talking about Byron as if he was a battery booster pack!

'What will happen to Byron when Gwen takes his future?' Siân asked. 'Will he die? He can't die!'

But Twm didn't answer. His head snapped up, looked at the open archway. His body stiffened.

Seconds later, Cassie and Siân heard the noise which had so startled him. Running feet, shouts, and a deep bass rumble, as though a large animal was in distress.

'The Helynt are coming,' Twm said. 'You shouldn't let them see you.' He stuffed his book and the open chocolate into the bag and scrambled to his feet. The girls were up too. The sound grew louder, closer, closing in on them.

'Up!' Siân said. 'We have to hide.' She pointed to the branches of the blackthorn tree above them.

The great branches of the tree spread like the vaulted ceiling of a cathedral. Its limbs were twisted, its thorns thick as pencils. The leaves it had dripped burgundy, bronze and brown. Could she climb it? Cassie wouldn't have bet on it, but the clamouring, cruel sound was so close there was no choice.

Siân gripped the lowest branch and hauled herself up, feet wedged against the solid trunk. One trainer slipped and kicked uselessly in the air. Cassie grabbed her sole and gave a solid shove up. Siân scrambled one leg over the bough. Twm watched them from the ground.

'Grab me!' Siân reached down and Cassie swung herself up, kicking and scrambling at the trunk for purchase.

Somehow, they both had managed to straddle the lowest branch.

It wasn't high enough. They would be seen.

Cassie edged towards the trunk, dug her fingers into the dark bark and hoisted herself higher. Her fingers pressed against something stuck in the bark — a piece of metal? A coin? It was hard to tell. And it didn't offer a good handhold. Onto the next branch.

'Be careful,' Siân warned.

Cassie *was* being careful. But it was difficult to manoeuvre herself in the precarious space. And it wasn't helping that, up close, the thorns at the far reaches of the branches looked as sharp as needles.

The dead leaves and twigs tangled close around her now. It was harder to see the root bed of the tree burrowing into the ground. Were they out of sight? Safe?

She stilled every cell and listened — owl-alert.

Siân crouched around the thick branches too, hiding from whatever was coming from below.

Then, the tylwyth teg flooded into the chamber with banshee wails, at least half a dozen of them. Cassie saw them flit across the small gap in the dry leaves she was peering out from. A creature swung into view. A derew, it had to be. But this was bigger than the ones she'd seen in Fiedown. Its shoulders were at head height for the Helynt. Broad and strong-looking, the derew reminded her of a stag beetle. Its body shone with the same dark iridescence, though this derew was shades of copper and bronze and gold. As it swayed back and forth, away from the Helynt, it trailed dancing streaks of gold as though it scattered tiny stars.

A tree spirit. She could hardly believe she was seeing such a thing.

But then she realised it wasn't just the Helynt who were shouting. The derew was shrieking too, almost too high-pitched to hear. It was in pain! Were they hurting it?

She clung tightly to the branch with one hand and, with the other, pushed some leaves aside to get a better view.

'Go left. Go round!' one of the tylwyth teg yelled at her companions. 'Quick, catch it.'

'Back up. Easy. Don't make it angry!' another voice called.

'Will, listen to me, go left, I said!'

The Helynt sounded angry, or desperate, or both. They yelled at each other, but no one was listening, and, in the centre of all the shouts was the poor derew, bucking and leaping.

She wanted to tell them to leave it alone, to leave it be. But the idea of being caught in Annwn and dragged before Gwen was terrifying. She squeezed the branch tightly, her fingers digging into the bark.

'Twm! Twm, are we too late?' a girl's voice called.

'I think so.' Cassie couldn't see Twm now, but he was down there in the thick of whatever was happening, whatever torment this was.

'What can we do? Shall I get Gwen?' the girl said.

'Yes. Hurry,' Twm's voice. 'Though there's nothing she can do either.'

The derew gave one almighty shriek that ripped through the air. Cassie wanted to cover her ears, but was scared she'd fall. She ducked her head instead.

What was wrong with the derew?

She peeked again.

The creature had curled up among the enormous roots of the blackthorn. It still keened painfully high. But its head was buried in its thorax, its legs tucked in underneath it, so the sound was more muffled. The bronze sheen of its body seemed to darken where its spine might be. A black line was forming. No, a crack was forming. Cassie could see it now. The two halves of its body were opening up along the centre line.

The poor derew!

The Helynt stepped nearer. One boy lay his hand on the creature, stroking it. His face was wet with tears.

Was it dying? Was this what Twm meant earlier?

One half of the derew's outer shell cracked and slid to the floor. The other side tumbled free seconds later.

The derew wasn't dead. It uncurled its head from its chest, stretched out its limbs carefully. It wasn't dead, but it was smaller. The creature that stepped away from the old body was half the size it had been, and its bronze and gold patterning was now more fawn brown.

Cassie pulled her arms and legs up and in, trying to balance out of sight. The bark smelled of soil and darkness and being buried alive, the smell of squirming. *Hold on, hold on tight. Don't fall.* Inside her trainers, her toes tried to grip the tree in terror. Shards crumbled free under her fingertips. Perhaps she had made a noise, because the crying boy at the base of the tree looked up.

And, as his eyes scanned the blackthorn, before turning back again to the derew, Cassie realised that she knew him. She had seen his face before.

The boy, who was definitely no older than fifteen years old, was Alun Wyn Roberts.

# Chapter 23

Cassie's mind spun like a Catherine wheel. Alun Wyn Roberts was standing beneath the blackthorn tree, crying over a poorly derew. He had disappeared fifty years ago and hadn't aged a day.

He hadn't been stolen and turned into a boar.

He hadn't even been stolen and grown old and died.

He had been stolen and kept down in the dark and had stayed exactly as he had been on the day he disappeared.

She looked at the other tylwyth teg. Gwen had taken Alun Wyn and turned him into one of them. He looked just like them, ragtag and dirty and so, so young. But he wasn't a real tylwyth teg! He had been a human boy before Gwen stole him from his family.

She clung tighter to the branch, a horrible, sick feeling made her feel faint.

*Don't fall off*, she whispered silently. *Don't fall off! And don't be seen!*

Suddenly, she wanted to be out of here. Away from the strangeness and the sadness and decay. Away from Gwen's influence. She wanted to be out in the fresh air under the sky, with room enough to *think*.

*I don't want to be here. Please get us out of here.*

She felt as if she was asking the tree. She pressed so hard into the bark that gritty flakes patterned her skin.

*Please, please, I don't want to be here.* A single tear dropped – *splosh* – from her cheek, onto the bough beneath her.

And she felt the bough, somehow, wake up. It felt, all of a sudden, as though she was sitting on something that knew she was there. The tree was as aware of her as she was of it.

A pale baby-blue finger of light rose gently from the bough, heading towards her. She wanted to leap away from it. Nothing good would likely come of tylwyth teg magic. But she was between the devil and the deep – if she moved now, the tylwyth teg below would spot her, and drag her to Gwen.

The blue light slid over her fingers, her hand. And, and, and . . .

She could barely believe it, though she was looking right at it . . .

Her fingers vanished!

Her hand too!

And wrist!

She wiggled her fingers, feeling the knuckles move, and the pressure of her fingertips on the bark still.

Her hand was still *there*, it was just *invisible*.

She'd asked to not be here, and the tree was giving her her wish!

She pressed tighter to the tree.

*Please, please, keep us both safe, don't let them see Siân.*

Her whole arms were gone now, her tummy and torso, and her legs were fading. She looked about. Where was Siân?

There was no sign of her. The tree had hidden her.

Or swallowed her.

No. She couldn't think that way. She had to believe that down here in Annwn, in the dark of the chamber, with the wild hoots of the tylwyth teg below, that something was keeping them safe. Anything else was just too, too terrifying.

'Cassie?' Cassie heard Siân whisper. She couldn't see her still, but her voice came from close by.

'Where are you?'

'I'm here,' she replied. 'But I can't see you.'

'We're invisible.' The thought was absolutely wild. 'We should get out of here while we can.'

'Yes. Stay close.'

Cassie inched her way to the trunk. She stood, carefully, gripping the bark, leaning her weight into the tree. It would be better to drop down on the other side, with the bulk of the blackthorn between them and the tylwyth teg. On the clamber down, she felt Siân bump against her once or twice, but she couldn't see her at all. Finally, they were back on the ground, in the shadow of the enormous trunk.

Cassie felt Siân, flapping her fingers, finding Cassie's body and clasping on, in relief.

'Are we still invisible?' Siân whispered.

'Yes, I can't see you. Or me. The tree did it.'

'I know! Pick up a stick.'

'Why?' Did Siân think they needed weapons? That wasn't good.

'To have a bit of the tree with us. To boost the magic signal.'

'OK.'

At their feet, the ground was littered with old, fallen twigs and sticks, the detritus of years.

Cassie picked up a gnarled, bent stick, fallen from the tree who knew how long ago. It vanished in her grasp. With her spare hand, she fumbled around, patting the air like it was a dog, until she found Siân's hand.

'Have you got a stick too?'

'Yes.'

Cassie hoped that the tree's magic would keep them safe, while the pack on the other side of its trunk focused all their attention on the derew.

They edged along the wall of the cavern, getting closer and closer to the open arch, and further from the tylwyth teg – the creatures who lived for ever in the dark.

# Chapter 24

They limped away from the dying tree, and back towards the tunnel. Cassie dropped Siân's hand so that she could dash angrily at her damp eyes, while still keeping hold of the blackthorn wand. Was she right? Alun Wyn was alive, but still exactly as he had been the day he went missing? The tylwyth teg had taken him from his home and made him one of them. He had been a boy — an ordinary boy whose family had loved him with all their hearts. But that life had been stolen from him. And he'd been dragged down into Annwn, never changing, never growing up. Never doing any of the things he'd dreamed he would.

Was that what would happen to Byron?

'I hate this place,' she growled.

'Me too,' she heard Siân whisper.

They followed the corridor in silence, up to the tunnel and out.

As she took each step along the gravel path, Cassie's foot and calf and leg slowly reappeared. The magic was wearing off. She could see Siân, first as a faded copy of herself, then more solid.

'What now?' Siân asked, her voice as tired and worn-down as Cassie felt.

'Home. Warm bath. I don't know. We failed, Siân. We didn't find out what Byron's gift was.'

Siân sighed. 'I know. But we do know what she wants him for at least – to keep the derew alive a while longer. Did you see that one break open like that? Like a snake shedding its skin. But the creature that comes out is smaller and weaker than the original. It's bizarre.'

There was nothing to say to that, so they trudged on together in silence.

At home, Cassie stumbled through the front door, with Siân close behind. Mam called out from the living room, 'Is that you, girls? Did you have your tea at Nain's?'

Oh, Mam thought they'd been at Nain's. Well, they had been before. Cassie decided not to mess with Mam's assumptions. 'We had snacks earlier, but not proper tea, no.'

Mam came to the living room doorway. As soon as she saw Cassie and Siân her eyebrows shot up like a startled hare. 'What in blazes have you two been doing? You're filthy. Is that twigs in your hair, Cassie? And you've brought sticks inside.' Mam plucked at Cassie's head, dislodging leaf shards and dried dirt.

They probably did have something of the scarecrow about them.

'Go and get cleaned up,' Mam said. 'Get a change of

clothes for Siân, if she wants. We'll have to keep a second wardrobe for her here at this rate.'

Cassie was about to thunder up the stairs to the bathroom, when Mam held out a warning hand. 'Byron's still sleeping. Don't wake him.'

After a warm wash, a hair brush and getting into her fluffiest pyjamas, Cassie felt a bit better. Not quite so sad and frightened. The cheese on toast Mam brought up for them a while later also helped.

She and Siân ate in silence, both feeling the warmth and tang of the food like a tonic. Cassie licked the grease from her fingers. Her mind had felt as tangled as her sock drawer, but, as she began to feel more like herself, she was able to sort out some of her biggest thoughts.

'Gwen used Alun Wyn like a battery pack, and she wants to use Byron the same way,' she said.

'It makes sense,' Siân said. 'In the books I've been reading the tylwyth teg often steal humans away from villages, but they never explain why. Turns out they use us as a power supply.'

Cassie wondered which of the children she'd seen were real tylwyth teg and which were stolen children. Then she realised it didn't really matter because the important thing was to stop Byron being stolen next.

Siân put her own empty plate on the bedroom floor, with the jumble of hairbands and gel pens and dropped T-shirts that were already there. She picked up the stick she'd carried out of Annwn, the stick that belonged to the blackthorn tree.

'And Gwen's like a witch, or a spider at the centre of a web,' Siân said thoughtfully. She rolled the stick between her palms then did it a little faster, as though she were trying to rub it hard enough to make fire. It was a bit irritating.

'What are you doing?' Cassie asked.

Siân twirled the stick in little abracadabra circles. 'I wonder if we might be able to give Gwen some of her own medicine?'

Downstairs, Cassie heard the front door open, and Dad's low voice growl a greeting. She didn't bother to reply — she was too curious about what Siân was saying. 'What do you mean?'

'Well, it seems to me,' Siân sat up a little straighter, 'it seems that what we have here, maybe, are two magic wands. The tree helped us, it made us go invisible to keep us safe. We've brought two bits of the tree home with us—'

'Two dead bits that had fallen on the ground,' Cassie corrected.

'Most of the tree is dead, but that didn't stop it helping. What if we could do magic somehow, to find out what Byron's gift was? We own straight-up magic wands, Cassie! The real thing. Not like those plastic ones my mam brought us back from London last year. Real magic. We were *invisible*.'

They had been. Cassie tried to hold on to the impossibleness of it. The total it-just-can't-happen fact of the thing. But it was like cupping air or plaiting water. It wouldn't stay put to be thought about properly.

Could they make magic themselves?

Dad's voice rumbled up through the floor. He sounded cross. A bad shift at work, maybe. The sound of the TV came on, too loud. Cassie wondered if Mam would warn him to be quiet for Byron too.

Siân jumped up onto her knees at the end of the bed. She held her wand upright, like a sword before her. 'Did you do anything, back in Annwn, when we disappeared? Did you say some magic words, or anything?'

A few days ago, this would have just been another of Siân's make-believe games. A magic potion made up of squished nettles in a bucket. But this was real. Cassie's tummy fluttered around the cheese on toast.

'I just thought about what I wanted to happen. I asked to not be there.'

'We just have to ask?' Siân was grinning now.

Cassie didn't add how frightened she'd been, how she'd clung to the crumbling bark of the blackthorn as though it was a life raft at sea.

'I wish for the power to fly,' Siân said, wand still aloft.

Cassie said nothing, but reached for her own wand, which she had propped up next to the bedside table.

'I wish for the power to hover a bit, then.' Siân had her eyes closed and her forehead crimped in concentration.

Cassie waited. Waited. Waited. 'It's not working,' she said. She hadn't expected it to, not really. You didn't get what you wanted just by wishing for it, everyone knew that.

'Don't give up,' Siân said. 'You always give up too soon.'

'No, I don't.' Cassie couldn't keep the narkiness out of her voice. What did Siân even mean?

'You don't have faith in yourself.' Siân was still staring hard at the stick in her own hand.

Cassie considered giving Siân a shove. Just enough to let her know she'd gone too far, but went for a glower instead. 'I have plenty of faith in myself. Mrs Khaleed always says, "Doesn't lack self-confidence" in my school reports.'

'She just means you talk a lot. It's not the same thing.' Siân lowered her stick. 'But magic doesn't happen if you don't believe in it. *Peter Pan* taught me that.'

'I do believe in magic. I've seen it for myself, remember?'

'I'm not talking about that, I'm talking about believing in yourself.' Siân held up her stick again. But no matter how hard she waved it around, she didn't move as much as one millimetre into the air.

# Chapter 25

Siân left pretty quickly after that. They hadn't rowed, exactly, but Cassie could tell that Siân was disappointed with her. For not trying hard enough, for not believing enough.

But that wasn't fair.

Cassie had done everything she could think of to help Byron. She'd asked him, she'd researched, she'd gone back to Annwn to bribe Twm. She wasn't giving up! She just didn't know what to do next.

From downstairs, the TV went suddenly quiet, as though someone had turned it off mid-show.

Cassie sat cross-legged on her bed, with the blackthorn stick in her lap. The brown bark was fading to grey in places, it had no magic in it.

'. . . what sick looks like!' Dad's voice was muffled but loud, clear enough for Cassie to hear his anger.

Mam's reply was too low to hear, but it sounded like an angry wasp.

'Lazy, he is, lazy and sarky with it,' Dad said.

Cassie hated it when they rowed. It made her feel as though her lungs were too small for the air she needed.

It hurt her chest. Mam and Dad didn't row very often, but when they did the house felt less safe, less certain.

They'd been rowing more lately. Without his Sunday walks with Taid, Dad's head was getting tangled up with cobwebs.

Cassie stood and went to the landing. If she sat on the top step, she could hear what Mam and Dad were saying more clearly, without being seen. It didn't occur to her not to listen.

'He stayed out all night, Claire, and wouldn't tell us where he was. When I was his age, I was already thinking about joining up, I had plans for myself. What's he doing, eh? Wasting his life. And he's got you running around after him like he is still a boy.'

Could Byron hear this? Was he listening?

'He is still a boy,' Mam said, her anger hurling the words into the air. 'He's *our* boy. Not that you'd notice for all the effort you put into looking after him.'

Cassie heard Dad gasp as though he had caught a tackle to his guts. Her own fingers tightened around the blackthorn wand.

'Well, if that's the way you feel about it.' Dad's voice was cold, hurt.

'Wait. Gareth, wait.'

Cassie scuttled back into her room, tears in her eyes, not wanting to be seen if Dad came out into the hall; came out and grabbed his coat and pulled open the door and stalked off into the night, and — what? — never came back?

The blackthorn had granted her wish down in Annwn,

when she was scared, terrified. Was that what it needed, the raw, bone-dissolving fear she had felt right before she had become invisible?

Cassie breathed in through her nose, feeling her nostrils flair. In her mind, she carefully opened the dark, secret place where she shoved all her real fears. The understairs cupboard of her brain, where the spiders and spooks lurked.

What was in there?

What was she afraid of, really?

If she was being most honest, she was afraid of Dad being gone, and Byron being gone, just like Taid. That they would both leave the place where they were both so unhappy. And that being that.

It felt dangerous to even think these things. It felt like an invitation. That somehow, by admitting what she was scared of, she risked making it real. She lowered her head, pressed the blackthorn wand to her chest, and screwed her eyes shut tight.

*Please make it all right.*

*Please let Mam and Dad be happy again.*

*Make Dad stay.*

*Make Byron stay.*

Was that enough? Had the magic listened? She opened her eyes. There was no shouting coming from downstairs. But that meant nothing. Dad might just have shrugged on his jacket and stalked off into the night.

She scrambled up to standing.

Cassie used the tip of the stick to ease the door ajar. Stepped through. Listened. Her bare toes clenched and unclenched the carpet fibres. Was Dad still here?

She had to go down and see.

As she stepped down, poised between hope and disappointment, ready to see Mam and Dad smiling at each other, ready to see Dad already gone into the night, she felt the stairway lurch. It *lurched*. She steadied herself on the bannister.

Something was happening.

The air looked different. She could see tiny particles of dust, floating the way they sometimes did in bright sunshine. But there was no sun, it was the evening. The bright particles glittered blue.

Some kind of magic was happening downstairs.

# Chapter 26

Cassie's left hand gripped the bannister, while her right hand held the blackthorn wand which had given her some kind of magic.

But what?

She had to go down and see.

With her heart thumping wildly against her ribs, she crept downstairs.

The light in the hallway was all wrong. It was night-time and the window above the front door should have been dark, but sunlight streamed in. It felt warm as she passed through it. Each step she took was more reluctant than the last. What had the magic done? Forwarded time?

With the tip of the wand, she pushed open the living room door. Here too, bright sunshine flooded in through the front window, showing up all the dust on the black TV screen in the corner. Where were Mam and Dad?

She was properly in the room now.

And there was her family squished around the dining table — all of them. Mam and Dad, Byron, Nain and Taid. Only her own seat was empty.

Taid.

Taid sat at the head of the table. His elbow propped amiably beside his plate, shirtsleeves rolled up, his skin tanned from long walks outdoors. His watch, the watch that was now Byron's, marked time on his wrist, though Taid always said moments like this could last for ever if you held on to them. Taid's hair was mostly silver, but his eyes were the same earth-brown they'd been in the photo on Nain's mantel, they hadn't changed since the day he'd married her. His eyes twinkled with the same fun and curiosity about the world as they had back then. He grinned as he reached for a bowl of roast potatoes and laughed at something Nain whispered in his ear.

Cassie couldn't move. Not an inch. She was pinned in place like the awful butterflies she'd seen once in the museum.

She could hear them now, the sound of her family. It was oddly distorted, like the deep echoes of a swimming pool when her head was below water. A boom and pop as Taid laughed. A swish and fizzle as Mam joked back. She couldn't make out the words, just the sounds of happiness, of being together with a good meal in front of them and an easy afternoon ahead.

Cassie wiped her cheeks.

This was a glimmer. A stupid *glimmer*. It was no more real than the beach Gwen had conjured for them in Annwn.

But, oh, it *felt* real. It felt like getting into bed when the hot water bottle had already made it toasty; it felt like clambering onto Mam's lap to have an ouch kissed away, it felt like . . .

. . . it felt like her heart was breaking all over again.

No one at the table looked her way. She was a ghost in a room full of ghosts.

Byron splashed gravy onto his plate. He looked younger, smaller. He wiped the lip of the jug with his finger and popped the spill into his mouth. Mam flapped at his wrist in mock horror. Dad watched them all, silent but smiling.

It's not real.

*It's not real.*

This was just a memory of a day, perhaps from last spring, an ordinary day just like a hundred others, when things had been solid and predictable.

She looked at the empty chair beside Byron. Her chair.

She could slip into it, take her place at the table. The strange sounds would become words, she sensed. She'd be able to hear Taid's terrible puns again; she'd be able to hear Nain flirt with him, even after all their years together. She'd be able to hear Byron's repulsed *ewwws* when the flirting happened, knowing that secretly he liked their closeness.

If she wanted, she could forget about the real Byron, lying sick in his bed upstairs, wasting away until Gwen took him for good. This could be her Byron, not the miserable, angry boy upstairs. She could join this glimmer family and stay in their light, in their warmth. She could pretend that nothing had changed. No wonder Byron wanted to go to Gwen, if Gwen could give him this.

At the table, Dad and Taid had fallen into a conversation about something so enthralling that they both waved their hands to make their point. What were they talking about? What had made Dad so animated?

She couldn't remember. This was an ordinary meal like so many others and she couldn't remember the details at all.

But, she knew, if she moved and sat down in her chair, then she would be able to hear them, join in, laugh at their eagerness, or take one side over the other. It would feel real.

And if it *looked* real, and *sounded* real and *felt* real, then who was to say it *wasn't* real? If she could smell the roast potatoes and taste them in her mouth, then weren't they *real* roast potatoes? Even if they were just a memory?

She could stay with this family, here on this perfect Sunday afternoon, for ever if she wanted. This could be her real family.

But as soon as she thought that thought, it felt like something heavy had charged into her. The pain of it winded her. She had a real family already. And they were sad and hurt and frightened and so often cross with each other and pretending wouldn't make that any less true.

There could be no more pretending. Cassie could feel a pressure growing in her chest, a feeling like there was a cat testing its claws on her insides. 'This isn't real!' she told the room. 'I don't want this!'

Cassie took the blackthorn wand, held it at each end, and rolled her wrists. She felt the stick bend at first, the tip pressing into her palms. She met resistance; it had reached the end of its bend. She forced her hands closer together and the stick, finally, snapped.

The air snapped too, as though it was an elastic band stretched too far.

And, in that moment, the world righted itself.

The curtains were drawn against the dark. The lamp was on, casting shadows in the corners of the living room.

Mam sat on the couch, looking at the blank TV screen; her hands were balled together in her lap. Dad, looking grey and tired with stubble growing blue-black on his jawline, slumped in his own chair.

The table, at the far end of the room, was empty, gathering dust.

'Cassie, what are you up to? Isn't it getting on for bedtime?' Mam asked.

'I heard shouting,' Cassie said. 'I came down.'

Mam got up off the couch and glanced at Dad before saying, 'It's all fine. Everything's fine. You should get ready for bed. Go, clean your teeth. I'll check in on you in a minute.'

Cassie allowed herself to be ushered out of the room, the broken wand still in her hand, and the memory of Taid's smile still fresh in her mind.

# Chapter 27

Cassie slept badly. In her dreams she was chasing Taid through underground caverns. She woke early and fretful. Before she went down to eat, she poked her head into Byron's room. It smelled stale. Byron lay on his back, eyes open, staring at the ceiling.

'How are you?' Cassie asked.

Byron glanced her way, then looked up at the ceiling again, apparently fixed on a thin crack in the plaster.

'Do you want some food? I'm getting breakfast.'

'No.'

'Tea?' She waited. 'Are you going to get up today?'

'What's the point?'

Cassie slid into his room and let the door close softly behind her. 'Byron?' she said.

He appeared not to have heard her.

'Byron? I wanted to tell you that I saw Taid again too. Last night.' She waited. Nothing. 'It was a glimmer. Like when you saw him at the river.' Did he even remember telling her about it? This Byron was more withdrawn, more sullen than even the most teenage of teenage boys. How could Mam think this was hormones? 'Are you listening? It wasn't real, Byron. It felt real, but I knew it wasn't. You have to know that too, right?'

She waited a while longer, to see if he would speak or respond at all, but Byron didn't even glance her way.

Cassie ate breakfast quickly and got dressed. The snapped blackthorn wand was tucked under her bed, where she had shoved it last night. She didn't want its glimmers, its pretending. It wasn't real. It was all illusions and shadows, and she didn't want the wand in the house any more.

Cassie found a plastic bag and dropped the broken stick inside. 'I'm going to see Siân at Nain's,' she yelled in the direction of Mam and Dad's room.

'OK,' Mam called back. 'Don't get under Nain's feet.'

'You saw Taid?' Siân asked a while later, her voice laced with unmistakable envy.

Cassie held the two broken pieces of her wand so tight that she could feel the bark flaking against her fingers. 'No. It wasn't him. It was a glimmer. A fake. It was bad. I want to get rid of the wands.'

They were in Nain's garden, sitting on her green plastic chairs. Weak autumn sun splashed lemon-coloured against the patio.

'But you did magic with yours!' Siân objected. She held

her own wand as though she were conducting an orchestra, waggling it in the air.

'I know. But it was all wrong.'

'Maybe you just weren't doing it right. We can get better at it,' Siân insisted. 'Practice makes perfect.'

'We're not perfect sort of people,' Cassie said.

'Speak for yourself,' Siân said sullenly. She held tight to her own wand as she glared out at the greenhouse and compost bin and empty clothesline with its fading pegs. 'I might get better at it, even if you don't.'

It was hard to give up magic, Cassie knew that. The very thought of it was exciting, like something from a movie. But it hadn't felt exciting when it happened. 'It wasn't *right*. I could tell that the magic wanted to make me happy, it thought it was good. But it was just a, what do you call it, a mirage.'

'Maybe we could use it against Gwen. Had you thought of that?' Siân suggested, obviously pleased with herself.

'She's been using magic for thousands of years. I did it twice, yesterday. Badly. It's hardly a fair fight.'

It was clear that Siân wasn't going to give up her wand easily. Cassie sighed. 'How about a compromise? We don't burn the wands, or anything drastic, but we hide them. Keep them safe, but not use them. How about that?'

Siân looked thoughtful, considering this. 'Where would we put them?'

'How about in there?' Cassie pointed to the greenhouse.

Nain's greenhouse was at the end of the tiny tablecloth lawn. The panes were kept spotlessly clean, so Cassie and Siân could see the workbench with its ball of twine and plastic muffin trays piled up for spring seedlings. One end of the workbench housed the sprawling geraniums, some still in furious pink flower, put in pots to spend the winter out of the frozen soil. It was neat and ordered and just the right place to put a plant when you wanted to keep it out of trouble. ·

'Fine,' Siân said, not even trying to sound happy about it. 'If you think we shouldn't use magic, we can put the wands in there. But I still don't see why we shouldn't.'

Cassie tried one last time. 'It's pretend, Siân. I saw Taid and everyone was so happy, but it was like a mask. The real world was hidden behind it, just as real as it ever was. The magic can make you see things and believe things, but it could never bring Taid back, not really. It's a lie. A trick. And we can't fall for it like Byron did.'

Siân held out her stick. 'I said *fine*.'

The greenhouse door was unlocked and there was just enough room for the two of them to stand side by side in the early morning warmth. This was Nain's haven, the place she had gone to most often when Taid died. She'd press her fingers into the soil and tease green fronds and leaves from tiny seeds. Then she'd sit in the sun rubbing lotion into her hands, her eyes closed.

'Should we tell Nain what we're doing?' Cassie asked.

'She won't be pleased we went into Annwn without telling her.'

That was true.

Cassie pulled a heavy terracotta pot from beneath the workbench. It was half full of soil, its insides speckled green. It was ready for spring bulbs, maybe — daffodils or tulips, something that burst with colour just when it seemed winter would never end. On one knee, Cassie pushed her broken wand into the soil. Siân added hers beside it. They stuck out like three straws in a glass of pop.

'Should we say something?' Siân said.

'Like what?'

'I don't know. People said stuff at Taid's funeral.'

'This isn't a funeral. It's a —' Cassie searched for the word — 'a retirement. We don't need to say anything.'

'Taid got his watch when he retired,' Siân said.

'Fine. Say something if you want.'

Siân pulled an empty sack from a pile near the back of the greenhouse. It was coarse and a bit dusty. Siân threw it over the terracotta pot and tucked in the edges. 'Goodnight, magic wands,' she said. 'I'm sorry we didn't get to use you much. Thank you for helping us get out of Annwn. Stay safe.'

With that, she pushed the whole thing back under the workbench. With any luck, that was the last they'd see of the blackthorn's magic.

# Chapter 28

Nain was up and dressed when they went inside the house. The small back kitchen smelled of hot chocolate and buttered toast. The fridge hummed in a friendly sort of way and the pale sun had managed to peep in over the windowsill.

'I saw you were here, Cassie,' Nain said. 'I thought we'd try a new hot chocolate I got from the Spar. It was on offer.'

Hot chocolate for breakfast? The day was already looking better. There was a small table, just big enough for two, pushed up beside the fridge. It had a wipe-clean tablecloth and a salt and pepper set shaped like a cat and dog cuddling. Cassie and Siân sat. Cassie cradled the mug Nain gave her and felt the hot steam dampen her nose. The kitchen felt safe. The window above the sink framed a sunshine-blue sky and the yellow leaves still clinging to the wisteria looked like lemon sherbets.

'What were you two up to out there?' Nain asked. 'Bit early for gardening?'

Cassie took a slow, slow sip of her drink, letting the

chocolate splash over her lip; she smeared her tongue over the creamy moustache, then wiped the lot with the back of her hand.

'Cassie!' Nain launched herself at the sink and dampened a cloth. 'Don't use your sleeve.'

Cassie caught Siân's eye — *question dodged*. She wiped her face clean of deliciousness.

'How's Byron today?' Nain asked.

'He didn't want his breakfast.'

'That can't be good.' Nain dropped the cloth back beside the sink and stood for a minute with her back to Cassie, looking out of the window. Should they tell Nain about the magic and Annwn? They had told her everything so far. Cassie felt a squirm of guilt — Nain had told them to stay away from Annwn. Nain's knuckles were pale as she gripped the side of the sink; her shoulders made a capital M shape. She was worried. Worried and frightened.

And she was right to be. Gwen still had whatever it was Byron had given her. And Twm hadn't been able to tell them what it was — they were no closer to rescuing him, or Alun Wyn, who, it turned out, was still alive.

Just then, Nain's phone rang. She kept it in a little knick-knack tray on the counter. Siân passed it to her.

'Sandra Thorn speaking,' Nain said in the voice she kept special for phone calls. 'Ah, Carys, su'mae?' Nain covered the phone with her hand and whispered to the girls, 'It's my friend Carys from the county museum.'

Cassie sat upright in her chair — for Carys to ring so early on a Sunday morning, she must have news.

'Oh, I'm keeping well. I've got my granddaughter, Siân, with me. Yes, that's right. Her mam's on a second honeymoon. I know. I know. Fuerteventura. I know! It was a caravan in Colwyn Bay in my day. How's your Pete?'

There was an endless, tinny chatter from the phone.

*Nain!* Cassie tried to glare her irritation at Nain, who kept her eyes fixed on the view from the kitchen window.

'Yes, Carys, that's right. Wait. Let me get a pen.' Nain opened the second drawer down, the one filled with bottle stoppers and loose straws and bag-ties and leaflets. She fished around until she found an old biro and a menu from the chippy. 'Right. I'm ready. Go for it.'

Siân leaned in, over Nain's shoulder, trying to see what she was scribbling. Cassie clicked the ceramic cat and dog together in frustration as the conversation went on with lots of 'Mmms' from Nain.

'Yes, yes, OK. I see. How do you spell that? No, this is brilliant. Yes, a trip to Chester sounds wonderful, I'd love a mooch around the rows. Saturday week? Great. Give my love to Pete. Rightio. Hwyl nawr.'

Nain tapped her phone and gave a sigh. 'Well, that's not good.'

'What?' Cassie asked impatiently. 'What did she say?'

Nain checked her scribbles on the menu. 'We were on the right track at the library. Gwenhidw is one of the tylwyth teg, the magical folk who live beneath the earth. The earliest tales go back thousands of years. Carys says there aren't many mentions of the derew, but that there are lots of stories about them under a different name — dryads.'

'I know about dryads,' Siân said. 'I read about them in the Greek myths! Sorry, it doesn't matter, carry on, Nain.' Siân held her face close to Nain's shoulder, trying to read as she read. The glittery beads on Nain's top sparkled in a sudden shaft of sunlight.

'Like Siân says, dryads are what the Greeks called them. But they were tree spirits that were worshipped all over Europe, once upon a time. In Wales the trees were worshipped by people called Druids.'

'I've heard of the Druids!' Cassie said. 'They have them at the Eisteddfod.' She'd seen them on telly. They were a procession of very serious people in mint green or pale purple robes who gave a throne to the best poet every year.

'No,' Nain said. 'The ones on the telly are writers and artists and the like. These were different. These Druids were priests. It was a religion. They worshipped the trees.'

Cassie leaned against the back of her chair.

'Carys says that when the Romans came, they crushed the Druids. They stopped them worshipping the way they wanted to.'

'Rude,' Siân said.

Nain tapped the menu with the tip of her biro. 'Well,

according to Carys, the Romans didn't like them because they sacrificed people.'

'What, like, killed them?' Siân gasped.

'It seems so.'

Cassie's mind tumbled with ideas. It was hard to know which one to grasp first. 'So, before the Romans came, the Druids worshipped the derew. Then, when the Romans came and banned the Druids, the Druids asked the tylwyth teg to look after the derew.'

'I suppose it makes sense for one lot of magical creatures to look after another lot of magical creatures,' Siân said. 'Gwen has been looking after the derew for, what, two thousand years. But they're getting sick, so she wants to steal Byron's future, she wants to take the years of his life and give them to the derew. Just like she did with Alun Wyn.'

Nain looked up sharply. 'What? How do you know what Gwen wants with Byron? And what did you say about Alun Wyn?'

Siân glanced, stricken, at Cassie. Cassie shook her head. Typical. Her cousin might be clever, but she had the common sense of a chopped log. There was no choice now but to confess.

'We went back to Annwn yesterday,' Cassie admitted. 'We thought we could bribe Twm to tell us what gift Byron gave to Gwen. He couldn't tell us, but he did say that Gwen is going to use magic to give Byron's future years to the derew.

We think she did that with Alun Wyn and she wants to do the same to Byron.'

Nain pressed her mouth in a fierce line and breathed deep with her nostrils flared. 'You girls weren't to go there. You have to promise me you won't take risks like that again. Anything could have happened!'

'Sorry, Nain,' Siân whispered.

'Sorry, Nain,' Cassie said.

'"Sorry, Nain", indeed. I don't know what you were thinking. Gwen is dangerous and you need to take that seriously. Carys told me something else you should know. Alun Wyn wasn't the only boy to disappear. She found a record of another local boy who vanished in the 1920s. He was reported as a runaway and it didn't make much news because of the confusion after the war and the flu, but his mother put an advert in the newspaper to try to find him. Another Penyfro girl too, that did make the newspaper, in the 1870s.'

There were more children, stolen — sacrificed?

Nain rested her hand on her chest, as though there wasn't enough air in her lungs. 'All those children, stolen, killed by that monster.'

Or.

A creeping thought fogged Cassie's mind. What if *all* the children in Annwn, all the tylwyth teg weren't tylwyth teg at all? What if they were all, once, children just like Alun Wyn?

'But Alun Wyn's still alive, Nain!' Siân said. 'We saw him. He's still the same boy he was when he went missing. He didn't grow up at all.'

Nain looked suddenly pale beneath her make-up. Her eyes welled with tears. 'That poor boy. His poor family. Mari grew up without her brother and he was still here all along? Oh, it's awful.'

Siân moved closer to Nain and slipped an arm around her, holding her tight around her waist. 'It's OK,' she said.

But Cassie didn't move. She'd been struck by something Nain had said. 'Mari? Alun Wyn had a sister? I didn't know that.'

Nain took a slow breath, steadying herself. 'Didn't I say? Mari Owens? Mari Roberts, she was back then.'

'Mrs Owens-across-the-way?' Cassie asked.

Nain nodded. 'Yes, it was her brother that went missing. She was a bit younger than him.'

'Not any more she isn't,' Cassie said. She thought of Mrs Owens, who was out most days, sweeping the seeds that dropped from her bird table, refilling and tidying for the small flocks of tweeting birds that visited every day. 'Poor Mrs Owens. Poor stolen tylwyth teg. No,' Cassie corrected herself, 'they aren't tylwyth teg. Only Gwenhidw is. What do they call themselves? Helynt. Trouble.'

How awful, that all this time Mrs Owens had been missing her brother with all her heart and he'd been so close all along.

# Chapter 29

'Should we tell Mrs Owens?' Cassie asked.

Nain moved over to the empty chair at the small table and sat heavily. 'What good would it do?' Nain said. 'She can't go and see him. Annwn is closed to those who haven't been invited. We can't get him back for her.' She dropped the menu, with its scribbled notes, onto the wipe-clean tablecloth.

'If Alun Wyn's anything like Twm he will have forgotten he even had a sister,' Siân said.

But it didn't feel right. It was more pretending, more lies — like the glimmers. 'Mrs Owens won't have forgotten him, will she?' Cassie replied. 'She doesn't know what happened to him all these years. It must be awful.'

Nain nodded. 'It was. I remember. She was still in primary school when he vanished. She was younger than me and Taid. She moved through the village like a wraith for years, poor thing.' Nain lifted her head and looked out of the kitchen window. Her eyes were on the pale puffy clouds that scudded across the sky, the crows that whirled on the mountain wind, but her mind was clearly back to when she and Taid were young, and Mari was the girl who'd lost her brother.

Cassie stewed in silence. Her heart was pressed right up against her ribcage, pounding hard. Her blood felt hot. 'It isn't right,' she said. 'It isn't fair. Gwenhidw is a monster who's been stealing children away all these years and no one has done anything to stop her. I don't just want to save Byron, I want to save all the children she's taken.'

'But how?' Siân asked.

That was the thing. She had no idea.

Cassie walked home the long way. She walked right along to the end of Nain's terrace and dropped down the road on the lee of the mountain. The pavement narrowed where an old chapel wall jutted out into the street. The chapel windows were boarded up, had been for as long as she'd been alive. The side road met the main road at a junction. She turned left, past the rugby club and Spar before swinging along the footpath to home. She wanted to clear her head.

Gwen had taken something from Byron one week ago. Whatever it was — even if it was as small as a hair from his head — had bound him to Annwn. He was weakening and weakening, forgetting who he was, snipping the ties that made him Byron Thorn, until soon, he'd go back there, never to return.

Gwen'd done it to Alun Wyn, and all the other children who were now Helynt. They weren't magical creatures at all. They were boys and girls who'd had their lives stolen from them.

By the time she reached her front door, Cassie didn't think she could feel any lower. But she happened to look over at Mrs Owens-across-the-way, who was out in her front garden, picking up fallen leaves. Though Nain said that Mrs Owens was younger than Nain, it was hard to believe. Mrs Owens' hair was a mixture of grey and white and brown. Without make-up, her skin looked soft where it wrinkled around her mouth and eyes.

For the first time, Cassie properly studied Mrs Owens, looking for signs of little Mari Roberts, whose brother had vanished. Cassie crossed the road, watching out for traffic.

'Hello, Mrs Owens,' she said.

Mrs Owens' front yard was stuffed full of plastic plant pots. In the summer it was a tumble of colour, the two metres or so between the house and the pavement was bright red with geraniums, pink with carnations, joyously yellow with fat daisies. Her bird table took pride of place. But now, in autumn, it was brown and moss green, with all the bulbs tucked in and sleeping.

'Hiya, Cassie-love,' Mrs Owens said. 'How are you all keeping? How's your mam?'

'Good, thanks.' That wasn't really true, but, Cassie wondered, how much did anyone talk about what was really happening. 'How are you?' Cassie wanted to ask about Alun Wyn, about whether Mrs Owens still missed him, still thought about him. Would she want to know he was still alive, still the boy he had been the day he went missing? Or would that hurt even more?

'Oh, I can't complain,' Mrs Owens said.

'Can't you?'

'Aren't you a funny thing? Well, I suppose I could complain about my knees, if you wanted to listen. They've not been right since I tried ballroom dancing for the over fifties.' Mrs Owens smiled gently.

Were her eyes sad, or was Cassie just imagining it? It was so hard to know the right thing to do – was it better to know something, even if you could do absolutely nothing about it? Or was it better to never find out and be surrounded by plants and birds and a neat little garden to be happy in? Would she want to know, or not? Cassie ran her fingers over the rough edge of the wall, feeling the fine grit and stones roll under her touch.

'Cassie!' Across the way, Mam stood in the doorway of their house. 'Cassie!' she shouted again, this time with a little wave.

'Your mam wants you,' Mrs Owens said. 'Say hello from me, would you?'

Cassie turned away slowly. It didn't feel right to leave Mrs Owens without telling her, but there just weren't the words to say what she wanted to.

'Cassie,' Mam said. 'Phone for you. Siân. She sounds frantic.'

Cassie picked up the pace and dashed inside.

# Chapter 30

With the thought of Mrs Owens, alone but for the birds in her garden, Cassie hurried into the house. The landline holder was on the kitchen counter, shoved in beside the kettle, but Mam was holding the receiver out to her. 'Didn't you just come from Nain's?' Mam asked, bewildered.

Cassie nodded and took the phone. 'Hello?'

'Cassie, you have to get back here, now,' Siân sounded breathless.

'Why? Is everything all right?'

'No. Well, sort of.'

'Is Nain OK? Do you need an ambulance?' Cassie thought back to the awful day in spring when the ambulance had parked outside Nain's house and Taid was carried out on a stretcher. Half the street had come out to watch. Mam had held Cassie back, to keep her out of the way. Dad had grabbed Byron and run back home to fetch the car so they could follow along to the hospital. Cassie's fingers tightened on the phone.

'No, we don't need an ambulance. Nain's fine. Get back here!'

'Can't you tell me—'

But the line went dead. Siân had hung up.

Cassie sprinted, well, ran and trotted as fast as she could, with little breaks for a fast walk, back up the allt road.

Siân was waiting for her, hanging out of Nain's front door with both hands on the doorframe, watching the street. She jumped down and yoinked Cassie inside.

'What is it? What's going—'

'Come, come, come, come,' Siân insisted. She steered Cassie through the house to the back kitchen and out of the back door.

Nain was already in the garden. She stood in front of her greenhouse.

Cassie froze, staring.

In the cold air, in a pot that was meant to be a winter bed for sleeping plants, something had stirred. Was still stirring.

A sapling, sturdy and solid, was growing up behind the glass. Its thick trunk had tipped the potting table over as its branches had strained upwards. The edge of the table rested against the glass wall.

Cassie walked around the greenhouse to get a better view. She slowly realised what she was seeing, and her skin prickled with shock. The wand, Siân's unbroken wand, from the blackthorn in Annwn, that they had hidden away in there for safekeeping, was *growing*. She didn't dare take her eyes off the sapling. The trunk — moments ago the thickness of

Dad's forearm — was swelling as she watched it. Soon, it was the thickness of Dad's calf.

Nain opened the greenhouse door.

The scent of spring surged outward, the smell of buds unfurling, tight-packed blossoms forming, and the green smell of growth. They could hear it too. It sounded like sheets of ice cracking, damp but solid, as branches divided and spread.

The top-most branch scraped a wooden finger along the glass roof. The pane lifted from its frame, wobbled—

*Crash!*

'Stand back!' Nain spread her arms, standing between the girls and the shattered glass.

The tree grew on regardless. It reached up through the broken roof, spreading like an opening parasol in a sunny beer garden, pleased, it seemed, to have the space to stretch, to have the chance to show off its blossom.

'Well,' Nain said. 'That's my greenhouse ruined.'

They watched for a few moments more. The sapling, now an established tree, seemed to run out of steam after its growth spurt. Its topmost branches reached the bathroom window. It paused, catching its breath. As it rested, the white blossom filled the garden with a Parma violet and lemon sherbet scent.

The ruins of the greenhouse, like a tent caught in a gale, drooped pitifully.

'Girls,' Nain said. 'Is there anything else you need to tell me?'

Cassie looked at Siân. Siân looked at Cassie. Where to begin?

'OK,' Nain said. 'I see you have more explaining to do. First things first,' Nain said. 'I'm going to clear up the glass. You two stay out of the way.'

'We can help. You need help,' Cassie said.

'No. I need help with some answers. I don't need help with broken glass. Not from you two. Go and sit in the front room until I've cleared this up.' Nain's lips pressed tight together, so Cassie could barely see the red of her lipstick. There was no point arguing.

She and Siân traipsed through to the front room. They could hear the brittle tinkle of glass from the garden as Nain collected up the broken panes. It was the only sound they could hear for a while.

Siân had settled into the comfy armchair, pulled Nain's crocheted blanket off the back and draped it over her knees. 'Is it the same tree growing in the garden as it is in the Thorn Hall, do you think?'

'What do you mean?' The ancient dry blackthorn in Annwn seemed nothing like the strong sapling outside.

Siân pushed her glasses up her nose. 'If one grew from the other, is it the same tree or a different tree?'

'Does it matter?'

'I think it does. If it's the same tree — which it probably is because it grew from a stick not a fruit — then is the tree in the Thorn Hall dead any more, if it's growing up here?'

This was the sort of question that Taid liked. The sort of meandering, twisting question that had no proper answer and made Cassie feel itchy.

'I think,' Siân said confidently, 'that the tree in the Thorn Hall wanted to come up here, into the light. And we helped it, without even realising. Like fate. Like destiny!'

Was that what the blackthorn wanted? Cassie cuddled one of the cushions for comfort.

'Right,' Nain said from the doorway. She was holding a packet of milk chocolate Hobnobs and she tore open the packet as she sat down. 'I need a biscuit for the shock,' she said, as she passed around the packet. 'It's settled down out there, for the moment. So, you two better start explaining.'

Cassie chewed while Siân told Nain about the blackthorn branch helping them to escape from Annwn by making them invisible. Nain listened, stunned.

Cassie took up the story when it came to what had happened last night. When she had seen the glimmer.

As she spoke, she wondered whether Nain would mind that she had seen Taid and Nain hadn't, but, when she got to that part, Nain surprised her with news of her own. 'Oh, I see Taid all the time. All the ruddy time!'

'You do?' Cassie asked.

'Of course. Your dad is the spitting image of Taid when he was your dad's age. And you've got Taid's eyes. And Byron has Taid's chin. And the way Siân sits when she's reading a book, with her shoulder hunched and her ankle tapping away? It's Taid all over. I see him everywhere, every day.'

Cassie wondered if Nain was about to whip out her sleeve tissue, but she didn't. Instead, she smiled. 'It's a gift,' Nain said. 'A gift from the world, to see him in all of you.'

Siân picked up the story again, right up to them deciding to hide the wands in the greenhouse. 'And you know the rest.'

'I suppose I do. I feel like Jack and the Beanstalk's gran. I know *how* there has come to be a magical tree in my greenhouse. Or do I mean *on* my greenhouse? But I have no idea *why*. What does it mean? What are we supposed to do about it?'

Cassie pushed her fingers through the chunky holes in the blanket she was cuddling. 'I think Siân's right. I think the magic doesn't want to stay in Annwn any more. The tree is dying down there, the derew are wasting away. We knew we had to set Byron free, then the Helynt, but I think it's everything. *Everything* in Annwn wants to be free. Nature doesn't want to be kept shut up, it needs to be wild!'

'And how do we make Gwenhidw see that? Will she let them go?' Siân asked.

'She has to,' Cassie said.

# Chapter 31

It was at that moment that Nain's front door opened. 'Sandra? Are you home?' It was Mam.

Cassie jumped up off the armchair. In seconds the little front room was a bustle of people – Cassie, Siân and Nain were joined by Mam and Dad.

What were they doing here?

Mam's face was blotchy, and she'd come out in her indoor leggings. Something was the matter.

'Byron. Is he here?' Mam asked Nain.

Nain held Mam by her forearms. It looked as though she was holding her up.

'I called you, but you didn't answer,' Mam said.

'I was out the back,' Nain said. 'What's happened? What's the matter?'

Dad pulled his fingers through his hair, frowning. 'Claire went up to see how Byron was doing. But he wasn't in his room. Wasn't anywhere. And he hasn't left his bed for days now.'

Cassie felt her stomach drop, a feeling like ice water sloshing inside her.

'Is he here? Did he come here?' Mam asked.

Nain shook her head.

'I can't believe he's done this again,' Dad snapped. 'What's he playing at? I tell you, Claire, if he doesn't start respecting us and his home then he might find he hasn't got one any more.'

'Gareth!' Mam's eyes swam with tears. 'You don't mean it. And, if you do, you want to be careful what you say about my children.'

'Stop it!' Cassie said. 'Stop arguing.'

Mam bit at her lower lip. Dad shook his head and stared out of the front window — as if there were answers out on the street.

Cassie searched out Siân. 'Gwen's called him back.'

Siân gave a tight nod.

'Who's Gwen?' Dad demanded. 'Is he running around with some girl, making us worried sick?'

'No. Listen. Byron isn't slacking, or wasting his life, or being a stroppy teenager. It isn't any of those things,' Cassie insisted.

'What is it then?' Mam asked.

'You won't believe me unless you see it. You'd better come out the back,' Cassie said. She eased herself past Nain and Mam in the doorway. 'Come on.'

They followed her through the little house, into the yard. The tree, in full blossom and standing as tall as the house itself, seemed to be stretching out with joy.

'What?' Dad said, looking up at the branches which had

definitely not been there the last time he had dropped off some shopping, only a few days ago.

'Your greenhouse,' Mam said, looking at the ruined structure and the panes of glass that Nain had propped up against the side of the house. 'Why did you plant a tree there?'

'I didn't!' Nain insisted.

The tree, as if demonstrating just how little control Nain had over its presence in her garden, gave a yawning, creaking sound. The petals of the blossom tumbled loose, billowing like torn-pillow feathers, settling to the ground. The yard was frosted with fallen flowers. And, like a fist unfurling, dark leaves spread from the boughs.

'No!' Dad said. He reached for one of the green plastic chairs, and dropped, heavily, into it.

'Yes,' Nain said. 'You two had better know what's been going on.'

It didn't take long for Nain to tell the whole story. Mam and Dad both sat while she spoke, watching the tree stretch out in its new home. Cassie could tell that they wanted to deny Nain's story, to say it was impossible, but — while the tree kept unfurling right before their eyes — it was hard to say what was impossible any more.

'So, you think that's where Byron is?' Mam asked in the end. 'In Annwn?'

'Yes,' Cassie said.

'And he won't be coming back?' Dad asked.

'No. Not if he's like the others,' Siân said. 'I'm sorry, Uncle Gareth.'

Dad's mouth floundered, open, but silent. Then he surged upright, and the plastic seat bounced backwards with the force of his movement. 'Well, that's just not happening. Not on my watch. I'm going to go there right now and drag the boy back by the ear, if I have to.'

Cassie stepped closer to Dad, looked up at him. She rested her fingers on his thick wrist, their tips pale against the dark hair. 'You can't, Dad,' she said as gently as she could. 'You won't be able to get inside. Only people who have been invited can see the entrance to Annwn. If you went there now, you'd just see the railway tunnel and path stretching out on the other side and the fields with the cows in. The path to Annwn won't be there for you.'

There was so little any of them could do, not against such ancient magic. Cassie was beginning to see that there was only one way for Byron and the Helynt and all the derew to be released from Gwen's clutches, and that would be if Gwen let them go.

She dropped Dad's wrist and walked to the new tree. Not a sapling any more, but a young tree with a long life ahead of it. She rested her palms flat on its trunk. Under the bark, she could almost feel the swell of life, rushing up like bubbles in a bottle of fizzy pop. She wrapped her arms around it and let her forehead rest for a minute.

This is what Gwen wanted to see, the tree well again,

healed and healthy. With her ear so close, the rush of growth under the bark sounded like distant singing.

'Gwenhidw has to let go,' she whispered to the tree.

'Cassie?' Siân asked.

Cassie turned to her family. Dad, angry and pale. Mam frightened. Nain worried. And Siân, who looked determined. 'Me and Siân have to go back to Annwn. We have to go straight to Gwen, and we have to tell her about the tree. We have to make her see that she doesn't need to keep everything down in the dark any more. She's been protecting the derew for two thousand years. Keeping them down with her. But that isn't where they should be. They were only shut in there because the Druids were scared of the Romans. That's right, isn't it, Nain?'

Nain nodded. 'That's what Carys says, yes.'

'Well, the Romans and the Druids are long gone. Gwen needs to let the derew go. And the Helynt. And Byron.'

Dad rubbed his face with both hands. 'I can't let you go down there. You're so little. You shouldn't be off facing monsters. I should be doing that for you.'

Mam took Dad's hand. Her face was still sad, there were still traces of tears on her cheeks. But she was smiling. 'We can't fight all the monsters for them, Gareth.'

'I can,' Dad said. 'I trained for it. I was a soldier, Claire.'

'We know. I know.' Mam reached for Dad, pulled him back to sitting and held his huge hand with both of hers. 'What do you want to do, Cassie?'

Everyone was looking at her. She felt her toes curl inside her trainers. All the grown-ups, the people she loved with a fierceness that surprised her, were looking at her to lead. Her mouth felt too dry to speak.

Then Siân stepped closer, to stand right next to her. Her funny, clever cousin who'd been with her all the way.

Byron, the Helynt, the derew, all needed her to speak. So, she spoke.

'It seems to me that Gwenhidw is the only real tylwyth teg down there. All the rest are children she's stolen, children whose youth was given to the derew. But I don't think the blackthorn tree wants that to happen any more. It wants to be up here —' the young tree's leaves rustled in the breeze and it sounded for all the world like laughter — 'I bet the derew want to be in the sunshine too — they're tree spirits after all. They've no business being down in the dark for ever.'

'So, we have to persuade Gwen to do the exact opposite of what she's been doing all these years?' Siân asked.

'Yes. She's been trying to hold on to the way things were. But everything changes all the time. People change. They're born, they grow up, and then they die.' Cassie looked over at Dad, who looked pale and unhappy. 'If we try to stop time, or stop things changing, then we're just playing pretend.'

Siân grinned. 'So, the plan is to go and tell an ancient creature of legend to grow up?'

Cassie shrugged, then nodded.

'What if she doesn't listen?'

'She has to listen,' Cassie said. 'We can tell her exactly what we've seen here. Look at the tree. Look how happy it is. She has to want the things she looks after to be happy. Doesn't she?'

Dad puffed out a heavy sigh.

Nain looked up at the sky. The sun had dropped in the west and streaks of pink and peach and purple arched over the rooftops. 'It's getting late. If you're going to Annwn to fetch back Byron, you'll do it with decent supplies and all the help we can give you, this time. I'm going to make you some sandwiches.'

'And warm clothes,' Mam said. 'I'm going to get your winter coat, not that denim jacket.'

Cassie felt her eyes sting with tears. Nain and Mam loved her so much she knew, they'd do anything they could to protect her. All her family would. Her fingers went to the rowan bracelet at her wrist. Even Nain's nain was protecting her though she had died long before Cassie was born. It was her wisdom that might do most to keep Cassie safe.

Dad sat still on the garden chair, looking at the tree.

Mam and Nain moved into the house, glad, it seemed, to have something to do.

'Dad, are you OK?'

Dad pressed his lips tight. Cassie was surprised to see his eyes were wet. 'I'll be fine,' Dad said. 'I was just thinking about what you said, about letting go. It's hard. Gwenhidw will find it hard, if she can do it at all. If she is even capable of doing it.'

'Don't worry,' Cassie told him. 'We'll get Byron back.'

# Chapter 32

Cassie and Siân were soon prepared for their trip down into Annwn. Mam came back with thick coats and woolly hats. Nain filled a backpack with cheese and pickle sandwiches, crisps, and bottles of orange squash. She also slipped a roll of Fruit Pastilles into Cassie's coat pocket when she thought no one was looking.

'Thanks, Nain,' Cassie whispered.

Dad had rallied too. He found a big torch and a spare set of batteries. He added those to the backpack. 'Take my phone too,' he said.

'I don't think there's any signal in Annwn,' Cassie said.

'Take it in case there is. There's an app on it that can tell you your position to within a metre. You'll know exactly where you are at all times.'

Cassie knew that what Dad was really saying was, *Make sure you know exactly where you are so that you can find your way home.* So, she took the phone even though she was certain it was no use.

When they were ready, they all headed out together.

The Sunday evening streets were deserted. Not a soul to

be seen. Even the birds were quiet. The colony of crows that usually kept up a racket on the top of the chapel were hunched down, silent in their feathers. It was as if the whole of Penyfro, right down to the animals, knew something big was happening.

Cassie and Siân walked at the front of the squad, with Nain, Mam and Dad following behind. It felt good to have them there. To know that they were wishing them on and would be waiting for them to return safely, with Byron in tow.

Cassie walked with her head high, her thumbs tucked under the straps of her backpack. Siân pulled sweets out of her pocket and popped one into her mouth. So, Nain had slipped a treat to her too. Good.

'Wan' one?' Siân asked, through chews.

Cassie shook her head. Her stomach felt too fizzy and bubbly to eat anything.

'What did you get?' Siân asked.

'Fruit Pastilles.'

'Same.'

As they dropped down through the narrow hillside streets, to the main road and round the estate, streetlights pinged on, casting bronze puddles of light. Behind net curtains, she could see lit-up front rooms, widescreen tellies casting blue flickers into the space. Penyfro was slipping from day into night.

Then, they were on the railway track, standing in front of the tunnel.

'Are you sure about this?' Nain asked. The grown-ups stood in a protective huddle around the girls.

'What other way is there to get Byron back?' Cassie replied.

No one spoke for a moment — there was no other way.

Then Mam said, 'I'm so, so proud of you. But . . . I can't bear to lose you all. So . . . if it looks bad, please come back.'

'Leave Byron?'

Mam gave a sob. Cassie could feel a lump forming in her own throat. Mam pulled her close. Cassie gave in to the hug, letting her forehead rest on Mam's collarbone, smelling the mix of supermarket soap and Olay moisturiser that was Mam. Her arms were a tight band, a band that promised love and strength and hope for as long as Mam was around to give it, and longer if Mam had anything to do with it. 'Just, please,' Mam said, 'please come back.'

Cassie and Siân walked hand in hand into the mouth of the tunnel. They were walking into the lair of a monster. Gwenhidw had stolen children away from their homes, without a second thought, and taken their youth, their memories and hopes and dashed them away for her own ends. Drips, like giant's tears, sploshed into dark puddles from the dark arched ceiling. Skitters that might have been rats, scratched and echoed from the walls. Cassie hoisted her backpack up onto her shoulders.

'I'm frightened,' Siân said.

'Me too.'

Siân squeezed her hand quickly.

Ahead, the path dropped, and they were soon surrounded by the sour, earth smell of the underground caverns and caves, and the detritus of two thousand years of hoarding. There was no need for Dad's torch, with the veins of blue light showing the way, but the weight of it was comforting, somehow, as though there was a part of him coming along with her.

Annwn. Cassie stepped carefully now, a mouse in a cat's bed.

Then, it occurred to her, if the plan was to find Gwen and tell her what had happened to the blackthorn branch when it was planted outside, then they shouldn't be trying to hide – they should be trying to be found.

'Gwenhidw!' Cassie shouted. 'Gwen!'

Her shout echoed through the winding side passage, bouncing out ahead of them into the wide central corridor: '—*wen-wen-wen.*'

'Hush!' Siân squeaked. 'What are you playing at? We'll get caught.'

'Good,' Cassie replied. 'The sooner we find her, the sooner we save Byron.'

She could feel Siân thinking it over: the horrible walking-on-a-knife's-edge fear where the thing you needed was the thing you were most afraid of. But they had to do it – it was their only hope.

'You know,' Siân said, quietly, 'you know I love you, don't

you? I know we fight sometimes and don't always agree, but you're like my sister.'

Why was Siân getting all mushy?

Because there was a good chance Gwenhidw would catch them, and erase their memories, and there would be no such thing as Cassie Thorn or Siân Price any more. There would just be two more girls joining the Helynt, two girls who would forget that they had ever been as close as sisters.

Cassie almost stumbled as she blinked away tears. Her family had changed shape this year, they had lost Taid, Dad had drifted dangerously, and Byron had acted as if he wanted to cut himself off completely, but despite all that, it still existed. It was real and it mattered. She gave Siân's hand a brief squeeze in reply. 'Don't worry, you can't get rid of me that easily. Gwen! Gwen, where are you?'

The answer came soon enough. As they stepped out into the milky-blue speckled corridor, there was the unmistakable sound of running, footsteps approaching. Four boys and two girls streamed from one of the side passages. Like Twm, they wore a strange raggedy hodgepodge of clothes — likely things they'd scavenged from Penyfro, she realised. Their faces were blank, thoughtless as empty jars. The tallest, a girl, carried a thick stick in her right hand.

Cassie held on to Siân's hand as the troop surrounded them.

'You are calling for Gwenhidw?' the tallest girl asked. 'What business have you down here?'

'I've come for my brother.' Cassie held her chin high as she looked up at the girl. 'I won't leave without him.'

'Who are you?' Siân asked. 'Do you know who you are?'

The girl smiled then. Her skin was freckled, Cassie noticed, as though it hadn't been so long since she played out in sunshine – how long had it been, really?

'I'm the Helynt,' the girl said. 'We all are.'

'But who were you before?' Siân insisted. 'Do you know? Do you remember your mam and dad? Did you have any brothers or sisters?'

The girl dropped her head to one side. The stick, which was nearly as tall as she was, rested against her forehead. 'I might once have had those things. I have some thoughts perhaps that there was once a table and many of us around it. But I can't recall any faces or names. If I can't name them, they can't matter.'

'Some things are better lost,' one of the boys added.

The girl angled her stick towards Cassie, turned it from a crutch to a weapon. 'And some things are better found. Like you two. Gwenhidw will want to see you.'

Cassie forced herself to take a deep breath, all the way in, then out – two, three, four – the way Mrs Khaleed had taught her to do when she was upset.

'Good,' Siân told the girl, 'because we want to see Gwen.'

# Chapter 33

The Helynt flanked Cassie and Siân on either side as they marched towards Fiedown.

Cassie had wanted this. She had wanted to go straight to Gwen and tell her what had happened to the blackthorn tree when it was given light and warmth and air, how it had burst with life.

But, now that it was actually happening, and the Helynt had them surrounded, she was scared that the news wouldn't be enough. She was terrified that she wouldn't be enough. She wasn't a hero; she wasn't the sort of person who made it into stories. She wasn't the sort of person who would ever get their own Wikipedia page.

It was too late to back out, though. And, if she turned and ran — the way that every inch of her body was screaming at her to do — then Byron would be lost. She had to make herself brave as best she could.

'Are you all right, Siân?' she said, loud enough for everyone to hear.

'Right as rain. You?'

'Never better.' She gripped her backpack tight to force her hands to stop shaking.

They passed the twin arches of the Tanglement and the Thorn Hall. Cassie caught a glimpse of the old tree between the marching bodies of her captors. It was so different to the flourishing, flowering part of itself that had taken root above ground. It was a heavy, grey, dry thing. More like rock than living wood.

Then, it was gone and Cassie and Siân were swept along to where Gwen was waiting, in Fiedown.

At the entrance, where the Helynt herded them through, Cassie tried to take it all in – but there was so much happening it was impossible. Like market day, like a grand parade, it was overwhelming. And the creatures present! Cassie felt her heart shrink inside her at the thought of taking even one more step.

The dank, cobbled-together-with-rope-and-ladders space they had seen before was gone. Instead, what was surely a glimmer had been cast over Fiedown. A grand staircase spiralled up the wall, its bannister a twist of gold and bronze. It was carpeted in red, and Helynt – boys and girls both – hurtled up and down, racing each other with glee. Their satin and silk clothes shimmered as they ran – much more like the tylwyth teg she'd seen in drawings. She could easily imagine wings sprouting from their backs to lift them up the storeys.

She wanted to search their faces for the one she was

looking for. But there were other distractions that demanded her gaze.

Derew.

Here they were. The spirits of trees and woods and forests that Gwen was charged with protecting in the belly of the mountain. Once they'd roamed free and wild, until people went and messed things up. Such strange beasts. Coloured, for the most part, like trees, in shades of emerald and bronze, they ranged in size from house cat to horse. The bigger ones had the brightest colours, the smallest ones were more drab, the colour of winter leaf-fall. Their bodies varied too, from the roundness of ladybirds to the sharpness of flower beetles. They had been decorated, like Fiedown, with garlands of petals and wooden beads. The Helynt who weren't racing around like children at a birthday party were tending to the derew, wiping their shining torsos to a sheen, combing filaments gently with their fingers. Getting them ready for something.

Cassie soaked it in. Music played from somewhere — whistles and strings and the thump of a drum. Helynt sang or shouted words, adding to the cacophony.

And at the centre of the room, sat Gwenhidw.

Her toes didn't touch the ground, her chair was so big. Stuffed and padded with cushions and throws, there was enough room for three people on there. Not a chair then, a throne. Beside her was a tall table, with a small silk cushion at its centre. On the cushion was a wooden bracelet.

And, almost hidden by the legs of the table, sitting on the

ground, with his knees tucked up and his hands cupping his chin, was Byron.

'Byron!' Cassie shouted, over the clamour of Fiedown. 'Byron!'

He didn't look her way. Could he not hear her? Or, worse, had he forgotten who he was? Had he forgotten his own name? As the seasons turned into years, turned into centuries, would he forget that he had ever had a home in Penyfro?

She tore across to him. Too quick for the guard to stop her. 'Byron, are you still in there?' She dropped down in front of him, searching his face. No bruises, no sign that he was in pain, but a blank look, empty eyes staring back at her. 'Byron?' she whispered. He said nothing. She grabbed his shoulder, shook him as though trying to wake him. But all she got was a small smile, as though he was meeting a stranger he was unsure of.

'No!' They were too late.

'Cassie?' Byron said, so quietly that she could barely hear him.

Her heart thumped back to life in her chest. Oh! He was still in there. Weak, but there.

All around her, the sounds of the cavern stilled. Drumbeats slowed. The Helynt quieted.

Cassie was aware that Gwenhidw had risen from her throne and was standing beside Byron's folded body, looming over them both.

She was going to have to look up. Look up into the face

of the only real tylwyth teg in Annwn, the source of all the magic and misery. Cassie couldn't move.

If only Nain was here. Nain and Mam and Dad. And all of the people of Penyfro — Mrs-Owens-across-the-way, Mr and Mrs Khaleed and the other teachers from school, Gemma and Tilda, the people from the rugby club and the chippy and the Spar. And all the families who had lost their children over the years and centuries that Gwen had lived beneath the mountain. The mothers and fathers and brothers and sisters who had never known what had happened to the child they'd loved. Everyone. All here with her to stand up to Gwenhidw.

But it was just her and Siân beside her.

She forced herself to raise her eyes, despite the worm-crawl of fear in her belly.

Gwenhidw, in a silver and blue dress that shimmered with fine seams sewn with slivers of magic, smiled at her. 'You've come to see your brother join his new family?' Gwen asked sweetly.

From her crouch on the floor, Cassie felt inflated, lifted up by her own anger. Byron's *new family?* His new family! How dare Gwen? Fury crackled in her heart, fizzing in her veins. Cassie stood up and glared at Gwen. 'Byron has a family already. He doesn't need a new one. I'm taking him back. Your family is just pretend.'

'Is that so?' Gwen ran her fingertip along the arm of her chair gently, as though testing its smoothness. 'And are you so used to getting what you want that you think you can step into my world and make demands of me?' There was humour in her voice, a kind of angry delight.

'I never get what I want,' Cassie said. 'Not really. I wanted Taid to get better, but he didn't. I wanted Dad to be happy again, but he isn't. New things have to wait for Christmas or birthdays. I'm not here to make demands — what would be the point?'

She could see Siân in the corner of her eye, listening to every word. Cassie pulled herself up a little taller, stood a little firmer as Gwen peered down. It felt as though Gwen was laughing at her, taking in every inch of her, scanning her face — and jeering at what she found there.

'I see,' Gwen said. Her smile didn't waiver, as though she found Cassie to be so unlikely a foe that it was a genuinely funny joke.

Cassie wasn't a hero. She knew that. She'd done bad things, cowardly things. Like the time she had deliberately broken Siân's dolls' tea set because she, Cassie, had never owned anything so neat and perfect; she had cried and cried alone in a toilet cubicle when a maths test had been returned covered in red crosses; she had lied and said she hated swimming — even though she loved it — just so she wouldn't have to show her arms and legs and the apple shape of herself to anyone. She wasn't brave.

But she could stand up for the people she loved. She knew she could. When Mam was tired after work and worried about Dad, Cassie would be right there with a cup of tea and one of her favourite magazines. When Dad had been at his most desperate, right after Taid died, and he had sat still on the couch and barely moved for hours, Cassie had sat beside him, just to let him know he wasn't alone. And she was here right now, wasn't she? She was here down in Annwn, fighting for Byron and all the others.

So, let Gwen look. Let her judge.

'I've not come to demand anything,' Cassie said. 'I've come here to ask you. Please, I want my brother back.'

All around, the children and the derew were creeping closer, stepping down the staircase, scuttling across the ground. They circled around Gwen's throne. It didn't matter which way Cassie stood, she had Helynt at her back. She felt the hairs prickle on her neck. Any one of them might leap forwards and grab her any second.

'Something happened that you should know about,' Siân said then. 'We've got news about the blackthorn tree.'

Whispers swept through the crowd, a wave of mutters and murmurs.

Gwen raised her hand sharply and the Helynt fell silent immediately. 'What news? Tell me.'

Cassie glanced down and back. Byron still sat, barely listening it seemed. He drifted further and further away from her every moment. She had to persuade Gwen to let him go, it was his only chance.

Cassie flexed her fists a few times to settle her nerves.

'We sneaked in here, two days ago, to see if we could find out what gift Byron had given to you that kept him trapped. Instead, the blackthorn tree in the Thorn Hall helped us. It made us invisible. We took two sticks to stay that way. When we planted the sticks above ground, the tree regrew. You should see it! It's huge already. It's bursting with life. It blossomed earlier today.'

All kinds of emotions stormed across Gwen's face — confusion, fear, wonder.

'It's alive, it's thriving,' Cassie continued. 'The blackthorn tree wanted to be above ground, not down in Annwn. I bet the derew are the same, and the Helynt. They shouldn't be down here. You shouldn't keep them trapped. Please, Gwen, let them go.'

# Chapter 34

Had it worked? Had Cassie persuaded Gwen?

It felt as though all the creatures in Fiedown, from the largest, jewel-green derew to the smallest, waif-thin Helynt, were pinned still, waiting for Gwen to speak.

And when she did, she dashed all of Cassie's hopes.

'What? You expect me to give up everything I've cherished, everything I've cared for on the say-so of a little girl? Humans can't be trusted. They fight and squabble with each other without a thought for other living creatures. They waste and squander so much, all the time. The Tanglement is filled to the brim with their rubbish and that's just one village. Humans are destructive. My derew will never return to that chaos. Who's to say you were even down here at all? You could be making up every word of this sorry tale.'

Cassie felt her body slump, her shoulders hang. She turned, searching the crowd for Twm. He knew they had been here. He'd talked to them, taken Taid's book from them. He could vouch for them. Her eyes scanned the faces in the crowd, but she couldn't see him there.

'I'll tell you what,' Gwen said. 'I'll give you a wager. Your brother is trapped here, coming back like a battered dog to its master, because he gave me something. Something that mattered to him. He gave part of himself with it, though he didn't know it. He's come back here to take his gift from me,' Gwen gestured to the wooden bracelet on the table, 'when he does, that will seal his fate. He'll join the Helynt for ever.'

Cassie's pulse raced as she looked at the innocent-looking bangle. Like the one she'd been given by Nain, it was made from pale wood, but this one had been carved from a thick branch and was embedded with glittering emerald green shapes. It looked a little like the skin of the derew.

'What's the wager?' Siân asked.

Gwen's hand hovered over the wooden bracelet, but she didn't pick it up. 'If you can find Byron's gift to me, then I'll keep this bracelet for another.'

'His gift?' Cassie asked. Her heart still leaping in her chest. They had been searching for days and were no closer to knowing what Byron had given Gwen than they had been on the day he disappeared.

Gwen gave an angry little smile. 'If he means so much to you, if he is part of your family not mine, then surely you know him well enough to guess his gift?'

Siân spoke quickly, 'It wasn't a hair from his head?'

Gwen laughed. 'No, of course not. The gift he gave me was something he loved, something he prized — it could hardly be a hair from his head now, could it? If you know Byron as well as a sister should know her brother, then you should be able to spot it in a heartbeat.'

A wager with the tylwyth teg.

'*Welsh Fairy Tales, Myths and Legends* says it's a bad idea to bet with a fairy,' Siân whispered. The stories Mrs Khaleed read in class held the same warning.

'I can't see another way,' Cassie replied. She dropped down to look at Byron. 'What did you give her? Please, please, tell me!'

But Byron's head just rolled onto his shoulders as if he was falling asleep or he'd drunk Nain's Christmas sherry when her back was turned. Idiot.

'So,' Gwen said. 'What do you say? Do you accept the wager?'

'What happens if we guess wrong?' Siân asked.

'Then you will take off those silly little rowan bracelets and put on my bracelets instead. All three of you will join the Helynt.' Gwen smiled horribly sweetly.

Her legs felt weak as pooled water, yet Cassie stood and turned to look Gwen full in the eye. 'I accept,' she said.

'Me too,' Siân added.

Gwen clapped her hands in gleeful delight. 'To the Tanglement!' she called.

The Tanglement? The cavern filled to the brim and beyond with the collected rubbish of centuries? That's where Byron's gift to Gwen was? It would be like looking for one particular snowflake in a blizzard. Cassie felt sick.

All around them, the Helynt gathered. Some had found drums and whistles. Others carried the smaller derew tucked under their arms or in baskets. They formed a bodyguard, or a procession behind Gwenhidw, Cassie and Siân. Even Byron staggered to his feet and took feeble steps after them.

'Cassie, are you OK?' Siân whispered fiercely.

It was hard to hear over the beat, beat, beat of drums, the clapping and whistling of the excited crowd.

'I'm OK. You?'

'I have a bad feeling. The tylwyth teg never play fair.'

'I know.'

The procession moved out of Fiedown to the central corridor. Even with so many of them, they barely filled it. Cassie saw Twm's face in the crowd, and Alun Wyn's, but there was no time, no chance, to ask either of them for help. She and Siân were on their own.

'What do you think Byron gave Gwenhidw? If it wasn't a hair?' Siân asked.

Cassie shrugged her shoulders. 'It could be anything. He's got lots of tat he loves. Comic book figures that I'm not allowed to touch. A postcard he got from a girl in Year Eleven who he said was his girlfriend for a while. It might even be his old teddy. He has one, you know. Mam says he couldn't sleep without it. I haven't seen Teddy Edward for a long time, now I think about it.'

She was blabbering. She did when her insides were jelly and there was danger on all sides.

'Come!' Gwenhidw waved an arm as though she were showing them the view from the top of a mountain, not waving at two thousand years' worth of rubbish.

It was impossible to see the edges of the chamber in any direction but the roof. And there were objects piled as high as the rock roof in places. Cassie wondered if the space was as big as a football pitch. Bigger, even. And the narrow lanes and wynds and ginnels cut through teetering towers. It was clear that there were different hands at work in accumulating the mess. Some of the tyres and wheels and bike parts were deliberately arranged, engineered to form sculptures that looked like working machines. Elsewhere, they were strewn as they fell. In other spots, they had been stacked according to size and function. In yet others, the parts were decorated with ribbons and wool bindings, looking like the backdrop to a play or party.

It was the work of dozens of hands over thousands of years. Penyfro's rubbish, scavenged by Gwen.

And somewhere, in this gargantuan tangle, was something of Byron's. Something which would set him free, if she found it.

'Can we both look?' Siân demanded suddenly.

'If you think that will help,' Gwenhidw replied.

'How long do we have?' Cassie asked.

'One minute for each year of Byron's life. Sixteen minutes.'

Then Gwen giggled maliciously. 'Sixteen minutes according to my clock.'

She pointed upwards. Hanging above the whole chaotic creation was a clock, kind of. It was strung from the ceiling and built of cogs and gears that had once been bike parts, pointing hands that might have been park railings, a face made of mosaic shards of plates and platters, long since smashed. The numbers made no sense. There weren't twelve neat sections, instead the clock face was scrawled with words like 'Winter' and 'Teatime' and 'Yesterday' and 'Never' and the hands spun backwards and forwards between them as Cassie watched.

Cassie's head swam with the madness of it. What did sixteen minutes look like on this clock? Did they have all the time in the world, or mere moments? She tried to take deep breaths, the way Mam told her to before tests or exams or walking in to somewhere new.

'Are you ready?' Gwenhidw said. 'Then hunt!'

Cassie and Siân stepped together into the Tanglement.

# Chapter 35

'Should we split up?' Siân asked, 'to cover more ground?'

The idea of being alone, with the whoops and war cries of the Helynt echoing from the entrance, was terrifying. 'No, stick together. But I'll look at the piles on the left, you look at the piles on the right. We split the work. If you see anything, anything at all, that makes you think of Byron, you tell me.'

They had to step carefully. Some of the towers of stuff were securely built, lashed tight with rope and ribbons; other towers were just thrown together, and the slightest knock would bring the whole thing crashing down on them. Gwenhidw's hoard of useless human flotsam.

The rag-tag pile of objects spread in all directions, as far as they could peer in the blue-tinged light. Like a museum given over to the oddity of humans, with a dank, charity shop smell, the objects rose in stacks. Dolls, dog tags, drills and dayglow socks; battered CDs, books, tattered racks of bric-a-brac towered all around them. Paths wove between the objects made by years of bare feet tramping. Cassie was amazed by the scale of it.

A teacher had once told her that Charles Darwin deliberately dropped coins on his lawn to watch the earthworms churn them down into the dark. This reminded her of that now. Gwenhidw and the Helynt were earthworms pulling the rubbish from the human realm down, down, down and stacking it high. Cassie prickled with shame at just how much rubbish there was.

Cassie searched; her eyes roamed up and down the left-hand walls as they walked. She'd noticed that there was something of a pattern to the piles. The stuff near the bottom looked older. The newspapers and magazines more yellow, more crushed together, looking like puff pastry on a sausage roll. It made sense. Stuff accumulated from the bottom up. She knew that from the pile of clothes on her bedroom chair.

'We should look up,' she told Siân. 'It will have been put here recently, whatever it is, so it will be near the top.'

They followed the narrow passage left, left, right, getting further and further away from Gwenhidw and the children.

How much time was left?

Cassie considered and discounted object after object: rusting toy cars; marbles shining like eyeballs in the press of stuff; the skull of a sheep or a goat. None of it said Byron.

What did say Byron? She'd lived with him her whole life, eleven years sleeping in the bedroom next door to his. But could she really say who he was? He was grumpiness and sulking and muttered sentences and grunts. But he was also the boy who used to run at Nain to be swept into a twirl when she lifted him off the ground. He was the boy who had wept and wept at the end of *Toy Story 3* when Andy said goodbye. He was the boy who still, to this day, wanted his mam when he was ill or hurting. At least he had been until Gwenhidw came along.

'What about this?' Siân held up a CD case, its cover cracked and scratched. It was Led Zeppelin. A band Byron liked, for sure.

'Not on CD,' Cassie said. 'The only CDs he has are ones Nain bought him as presents. His music's on his phone.'

'Oh, I wonder if he gave Gwenhidw his phone? He loves that,' Siân suggested.

He did love it. Cassie held the idea of Byron on his phone for a second, the way he crouched over it, shutting her out, the way Dad told him off for checking it at Sunday dinner. He cared about it a lot. But was it the thing he cared about most of all? She didn't believe that, not really.

Cassie stopped walking. Siân, who had been peering at an unlikely pile of twisted bike wheels and plaited blue ropes, stopped too. 'What? Do you think you know what he gave Gwen?'

'No. But I know that I'll recognise it as soon as I see it. The same way I'd recognise him, even if I hadn't seen him in years. We need to look faster!' Cassie stepped off again, her pace quicker this time. She didn't need to look at every single thing and weigh up the chances of it belonging to Byron — she was certain that when she saw the right object, it would leap out like a jack-in-the-box.

She whirled past a stack of cupboards, balanced one on top of the other, some doodled and painted on by one of the Helynt with years and years of time on their hands. None of these things had anything to do with Byron.

'Why does she keep all this junk?' Siân toed a broken doll's pram, with a lopsided Barbie doll splaying its limbs inside.

Cassie shook her head. 'It's not junk to Gwen. It shouldn't be junk to people either. But it got thrown out. Chucked, instead of mended. She's had the Helynt cleaning up after humans for centuries. No wonder she's cross with us. No wonder she doesn't trust us.'

'Do you trust her?' Siân asked.

'What choice is there? Come on, let's keep looking.'

Deeper and deeper into the Tanglement they went. The piles here were weighed down and spreading with the density of themselves, congealing into almost solid blocks of grey and brown and weak-tea yellow.

'Halfway!' Twm's voice shouted, loud enough for Cassie and Siân to hear.

Halfway?

There wasn't enough time. If they didn't find Byron's gift soon, then they would join him and become one of the memoryless, familyless Helynt that haunted Annwn with their mischief.

They wouldn't see Nain or Mam or Dad again. She would never know whether Gemma was having a baby girl or boy;

never find out if Mrs Khaleed would ever persuade Mr Khaleed that he could learn Welsh if he put his mind to it; never watch Penyfro Rugby win the league. The village would carry on, but without Cassie or Siân as part of it. Mrs Owens-across-the-way would have two more children to mourn.

And that wouldn't be the end of it.

Before too long, the derew would weaken once more and Gwenhidw's eyes would roam upwards again. Another child from Penyfro would be invited down into Annwn, then another and another — for ever.

'We have to find it. We have to get out of here,' Cassie said, urgently. She followed the path, winding in and around on itself — an enormous charity shop of *stuff*, a giant jumble sale, heaps and heaps of . . . just *rubbish!*

She felt her heart racing now. She broke into a run. Where was it? *Where was it?* There was no time left.

Behind her, Siân ran too. 'Wait, wait for me. Where are you going?'

Cassie spun around, careful not to knock cracked china plates off dirty old dressers, or eyeless teddy bears from dusty, grimy shelves. Then, between a broken-down bookcase and a pile of red plastic crates, she saw a narrow opening, a gap where the earth was bare, and a black shape crouched. What was that?

Why was there a break in the tangled chaos here? Why wasn't this space, like all the rest, stuffed full of Gwenhidw's strange collection?

Cassie reached into her backpack and pulled out the torch Dad had given her. In its strong beam she saw that the black shape was a narrow cave opening, just big enough for a child to creep inside, if they were curious.

'Hey, Siân. Over here.' Cassie dropped to all fours and wriggled her way into the gap.

# Chapter 36

Cassie and Siân were inside a cave. It was the first truly human-sized space they had come across in Annwn. Unlike the cavern of Fiedown or the huge, vaulted corridors that connected Fiedown to the Tanglement and the Thorn Hall, this space was tiny. Roughly the same as Cassie's bedroom back home, it had enough room for a single bed and a narrow cupboard and not much else. And it had been someone's bedroom, once upon a time, although it had clearly been abandoned long ago. There was a low wooden frame, the torn mattress stuffed with ancient hay that was more dust than straw. A blanket of grey wool, threadbare and pocked with holes, had been thrown over the little bed. Like the corridor its walls were scrawled with hundreds of dark pictures, though these were almost miniatures.

'Whose room is this?' Siân asked. She could just about stand without banging her head on the ceiling.

Cassie flashed Dad's torch from the bed, to the walls and back again.

'What was that?' Siân asked. She pointed to the wall.

Cassie scrambled for Dad's phone and switched on its

torch. She gave the big beam to Siân who swept light in a wave across the drawings. At the centre of the image was a stick figure with long hair – a little girl. Around her was a small tree, a group of taller men. Then three beetle-like creatures almost the height of the tree.

'Gwenhidw?' Siân asked. 'Do you think those men are the Druids, coming to ask her to take care of the derew?'

Was there time for this? Cassie wanted to go back to the maze. Byron's gift wasn't in here. But there was something mesmerising about the drawings. They repeated, she realised. There was the girl again, down by the ground. There were the men, again and again, near the bed, near the door, near the ceiling. Each time they were drawn more wildly, the strokes dashed against the rock without care.

If Gwen had drawn these images, she had done it again and again, getting angrier each time.

Cassie reached out and rested a finger on the sooty black marks. 'Was this where she lived, do you think? Before she captured the first Helynt?' The bed was so small, so sad-looking.

'I think this was her home once,' Siân said. 'And she started collecting all the objects out there around this spot. This is the centre of the Tanglement.' Siân followed a particularly wayward scrawl down towards the ground, where her beam came to rest on a small object. She bent down and scooped it up. It sat squat on the palm of her hand.

Siân held a metal horse, dark with grime and time, with four small wheels where its hooves should be. There was little detail, no features on its face, it had no mane or tail, but the curved shape of a black stallion was unmistakable. Siân turned one of the wheels gently with her finger and it squeaked wanly. It looked old, perhaps as old as Gwenhidw herself.

'Is it a toy?' Cassie asked. 'A toy horse?'

Siân pressed a small catch on the horse's belly and a tiny metal door fell open, revealing a hollow inside. 'I think it's the Trojan horse,' Siân said. 'The one from the old story. Do you remember?'

'Why would Gwen have a toy Trojan horse?'

Siân shook her head and spun one of the wheels again. 'I don't think it belongs to Gwen. Or at least, maybe it does now . . .'

'What do you mean?'

Siân's eyes widened in the torchlight, her eyebrows shot up. 'I reckon this was Twm's once upon a time. Maybe this is what he gave to Gwen as his gift. We know that story means the world to him. I think this is the thing that keeps Twm trapped in Annwn.'

Cassie shrugged. She bent down, to be able to fit back through the cave mouth into the towering chaos of the Tanglement. 'Maybe it is, but it's Byron's gift we're looking for. Come on.'

Siân followed her back out. 'Wait. Listen. Twm was the very first of the Helynt, he told us so when we first met him. If we free him, if he gets his memories back, then maybe he can help all the others remember who they are. We might be able to free all of the Helynt, not just Byron.'

It was too risky. 'What if it isn't his gift? What if it's just some old toy that got brought down here with all the other rubbish?'

Siân thrust it out to her. 'Hold it. Feel it. It feels so fragile. It's ancient, Cassie. And this is a real plan, one that we know we can try. If we hunt for Byron's gift and don't find it that will mean we're *all* stuck down here in Annwn.'

Cassie folded her arms. How could Siân give up on Byron now? 'It's not what we're here for. It isn't Byron's, is it?' She turned her back on Siân. 'We're running out of time. Help me look, Siân!'

They were in the centre of the Tanglement. The spread of objects loomed in every direction. Somewhere, in the midst of all this mess, was something Byron treasured more than anything. But what was it? Where was it? All the confidence she'd felt earlier had drained out of her, and she felt doomed to see the time slip away.

She saw Byron again, in her mind, standing on the edge of Penyfro Mountain with the sad bleats of sheep in the air and the cold wind cutting at the seams of them. He'd said then that he was lonely. And he was right. She didn't know him at all. This proved it.

He'd held his hands to his head in despair, his wrists pale and—

Wait.

His wrists had been bare. She was certain of it. And when she'd tried to push the rowan bracelet over his hand, his wrist had been bare then too.

'His wrist!' Cassie shrieked.

'What?'

'Taid's watch. It's the thing Byron treasures more than anything. Dad gave it to him when Taid died. And he wore it every day. But he wasn't wearing it when I forced him to walk up the mountain with me. I remember that I noticed the scratches on his wrists where he'd clawed at himself. But I didn't realise until this second what that means: his wrists were bare! He gave Gwenhidw Taid's watch – I bet he did.' She was right, she knew it. She felt exhilarated, as though she might lift up and fly over the Tanglement. She was right!

But that didn't mean that she knew where it was.

'Three minutes left!' Twm's voice echoed loudly from the entrance. Gwen's clock was ticking down too.

'We have to look for the watch,' Cassie said.

'No. We have to get back and give Twm his gift back.' Siân held up the toy horse.

'Time's running out! I don't want to give up.' Cassie's chest felt tight, as though the dust and dampness of the Tanglement blocked her lungs. She couldn't give up on Byron.

'We aren't giving up,' Siân reached for Cassie's shoulder with her free hand. She pulled her closer until their foreheads were touching. 'Cassie. Listen. We aren't giving up. We're doing what we can with what we've got. If we leave now, we might get back in time to save Twm. He might help us save the others. If we wait, then time will run out and we'll have nothing.'

Cassie leaned against her cousin. 'It feels like giving up.' The thought of Mam and Dad and Nain, waiting for them at the tunnel entrance, relying on them to rescue Byron, was breaking her heart. What if none of them ever came back?

'Cassie,' Siân said. 'We have to decide, and we have to decide right now.'

# Chapter 37

'One minute left,' Twm's voice shouted.

Cassie had one minute to decide what to do: keep looking for Byron's watch, or take the toy horse out of the Tanglement. If Siân was right about it belonging to Twm, then freeing him might bring him over to their side.

But what if Siân was wrong?

What if it was just a toy horse that meant nothing to no one, and had just been scavenged with the rest of the rubbish down here?

'Is it really our only shot?' she asked Siân. Soon, very soon, she might not remember Nain's face, she might not remember her red-lipped smile or the way that she always slipped a little treat into Cassie's pocket when she thought Mam wasn't looking.

She might be about to lose her memories, but there was a real chance that they could save Twm, if nothing else. If that's all they could do, was it enough?

'Run!' Cassie said.

They rushed back the way they had come, barely glancing

at the tottering trash towers, the melee of objects and memories. How much time was left?

'Twenty seconds,' Twm's voice echoed above them.

'Faster!' Cassie gasped.

Were they even headed the right way? Had she seen that pile of dolls' prams and broken climbing frames before? Or were they a new pile of lost things?

'Ten, nine, eight—' the sound of a dozen other voices clamoured as the other Helynt joined Twm's countdown.

'There!' Siân pointed to the wayward clock that hung above the entrance. Nearly there!

With one last burst of speed, the two girls tumbled headlong out of the Tanglement and fell in a sprawl at Gwen's feet.

'One!' Twm cried and the clock let out a sharp burst of tuneless chimes.

Gwenhidw stood flanked by the children she had stolen from the world above, boys with knot-riddled hair, and girls with dirt beneath their nails and in the creases of their knuckles. Derew gathered nearby too, huddled in tight groups like sheep in a pen.

'What gift have you brought for poor Byron?' Gwenhidw said. Her eyes were focused on the dark peep of metal visible between Siân's fingers. Gwen smiled, the corner of her mouth clearly amused at their choice. 'Is *that* what you think your brother cherishes most in the world?' She started laughing as though they had told her the best joke.

Siân took one step forwards, another.

Then turned from Gwenhidw and Byron both. She lurched urgently up to Twm. Pulled his hand to hers. Pressed the toy horse into his palms. 'I think this is yours,' she said.

Twm looked wildly from Siân to Gwen and back again. He shook his head.

'No, no, no.'

But it wasn't Twm who spoke, it was Gwenhidw. Her voice was sharp, not laughing at all now.

'Remember, Twm!' Cassie urged him. 'Remember who you were.'

Something was happening, as Twm held the little model of the Trojan horse. 'This was mine,' he whispered. 'This was the toy I played with. Pater gave it to me. It came from the market at the fort. Pater told me about the Greek warriors. Pater told me about Troy. I remember!'

In the cavern, in the darkness he had lived in for two millennia, Twm shook with the shock of what he was remembering. His mater and pater. He had once had a mater and pater. 'I was their son!' he cried. And the sound of it could have wrenched the hardest heart in two.

As if answering Twm's shout, blue light from the glowing veins of the ceiling sank down towards him. It twisted and took on a distinct shape — a man and a woman. Ghostlike forms, glowing and transparent, came to rest beside him. The woman, who looked so like Twm, though her face was lined and older, held open her arms in invitation.

Twm gave a strangled sob and staggered towards his mater. But, where their arms should have met, flesh on flesh, instead Twm slipped right through her glowing shape. The toy horse dropped to the ground with a clang.

The woman looked shocked.

Twm's pater held her up as she reached again, and again, for Twm, but her hands passed right through his body, insubstantial as smoke. Cassie could see tears glistening on his mother's cheeks. She had waited so very long, and still she couldn't touch her son.

Twm let the woman, his mother, *un*touch him. He accepted her not-there strokes with a stillness that almost hummed with need. But, Cassie thought, it was like drinking from an empty glass. There was no comfort in it.

Twm pressed his own hands to his face, covering his eyes. Then wrenched them away to face Gwenhidw, full of fury. 'You stole me away from my mater and pater!' Twm hurled the words at her. 'They wanted me, and you made me forget about them. I'm not Twm. I'm Autumus Gallus, son of Lucian Cornelius Gallus, who was born in Syria before joining the legions of Rome.'

Behind him, the shade of Lucian Cornelius Gallus, Twm's father, held his mother upright, as she wept. They could all see her lips wailing, but her pain was soundless. She couldn't touch Twm with her words either.

'How could you?' Twm asked Gwen.

Gwen stepped back, moving away from Twm's anger.

She held up her hands. 'I had been alone for so long. Then you came here. *You* came to *me*,' she stressed.

Twm's face flickered, mouth frowning. He was remembering, Cassie realised.

'I found a cave,' Twm said. 'I was playing at being Odysseus in the cyclops' lair, and I saw you. You were lonely, so I gave you my toy and you gave me a bracelet. We exchanged gifts. And then I forgot who I was.'

He turned back to his parents. His mother reached out and attempted to stroke his face, touch his cheek, but her fingers were no more than mist.

'Why can't she touch me?' Twm threw the question out like a wounded dog might whine.

A stir went through the ranks of the gathered children, as if they too were injured.

'It isn't fair!' He turned to the crowd. 'None of this is fair.'

Cassie couldn't hold back any longer. 'Twm,' she called, 'Twm, do you remember where Byron's gift is?'

The question fell like raining embers on the Helynt, sparking more questions. 'What was my gift?' one girl asked. Then more voices, 'What did I give?'

'Who am I?'

'What's my name?'

Twm spun in a circle, searching out a face. 'You!' he pointed to a girl with red-brown hair and a scattering of freckles. 'You came here second. Fifty seasons after me.

You're Bridget. You had a corn doll tied with a green ribbon. It's part of the Dolly Wall.'

Bridget's face flickered with recognition. Then she tore off into the Tanglement, clearly sure where she was headed.

Twm grabbed another boy. 'You're William. You came here between two of the bigger wars. You had a knitted dog. It's in the chest with the carved sea monsters.'

William whipped off after Bridget.

'You're Alun Wyn Roberts. Your gift was a small penknife. One of the toy soldiers has it as a bayonet.'

Soon the other children were clamouring, yearning, demanding answers from Twm. They rushed in and out of the Tanglement. From the ceiling, Cassie could see more and more sparks of blue light, shapes starting to form. Parents, too many to count, searching out the child they had lost, decades, centuries ago. There were Victorian women in corsets and bonnets, their faces anxious as they looked for their boy, their son in the crowd. Peasant farmers in faded, patched smocks moved restlessly, eyeing each face with shrewd appraisal — was their daughter here? Earlier ghosts, in tunics and sandals, Viking maybe, or Saxons?

Aeons and ages of parents.

Mams and tads, paters and maters, mamas and papas. People whose love had kept them tethered to the world, hoping that one day they would see the face of their child one last time. And they searched, they hunted. Knowing exactly what they yearned to see, the shade of an eye, the shape of a nose — the child they had lost, found at last.

And when they found them.

Oh.

Cassie could feel the depth of what it meant. Ghostly blue hands reached for cheeks, for shoulders, but passed, like fog, through the bodies of their children. Everywhere, moans from the Helynt that were part-joy, part-grief, echoed off the cavern walls.

'Why can't I touch them?' Twm wailed again.

Cassie looked for Gwenhidw, looked for the person who had caused all this pain. Where was Gwenhidw, queen of the tylwyth teg? And, Cassie realised in panic, where was Byron?

# Chapter 38

Cassie dashed between crying Helynt, floating parents, the overspill of the Tanglement as children tossed objects aside looking for their own gifts. Where was Gwen and where was Byron?

'Twm!' Siân called. 'Where did Gwenhidw go?'

But he didn't even look her way. He gazed at the ghostly blue shape of his mother, seemingly spellbound. She and his father gazed back, unable to touch his face, his hands, unable to hold him tight.

'Cassie, wait for me,' Siân shouted.

'Where would she go?' Cassie asked Siân.

They scanned the wide corridor. Would she head back to Fiedown and the glimmer she'd created there? Or down one of the side tunnels into the warren of the earth? Or even out to Penyfro?

Then they heard a shout coming from the Thorn Hall. It was a shout that was full of misery and heartache.

'That way!' Cassie said.

She and Siân both raced away from the Tanglement, across the wide corridor and under the huge arch into the Thorn Hall.

Before them was a painful sight. Gwenhidw, Byron, a few forlorn-looking derew and the blackthorn tree.

The tree was unquestionably dead.

It had shed all its leaves and the bare branches were grey and dry. It looked like a tree cast in concrete, not something that had grown from a sapling to the enormous size it was now. Even its thorns looked brittle.

Gwenhidw stood, with both palms resting on its trunk, Byron lay still, propped up between its thick roots. It was Gwen's keening they could hear, her grief for the tree.

The half dozen derew blinked their dark eyes, pressed their bodies together for comfort as the person who was supposed to care for them sobbed.

Cassie edged into the space. Was Byron alive? Was he still Byron or had they already lost him? She was relieved to see that his wrists were still bare.

'Byron!' Cassie whispered.

At the base of the tree, Gwen whirled around to face them. 'Stop! Not one step closer. You think you can come to my home and destroy everything? I won't have it, do you hear? I won't.'

Cassie realised with a start that Gwen's face was wet with tears. She hadn't expected crying, despite the noise Gwen was making. Real tears seemed too human, somehow.

'If I am to fail . . .' Gwen paused. Her eyes lifted to the dead branches above her. 'If I am . . .' She wiped her face with the back of her sleeve. The dress, which had looked so beautiful earlier, was a dull grey. Gwen's tears stained the fabric. 'If I am to lose *everything,* then so will you.' Her voice rose, 'None of you will ever leave here. I will tear down every entrance and seal every tunnel before I let a single one of you go.'

Cassie glanced behind her. There were more children in the room now: beside her and Siân, the Helynt had crept in, silently, their faces filled with anger at their captor. The ghostly parents accompanied them, unwilling to be parted for even a second, though they were not reunited, not really.

Cassie's heart, already wrung out and sore from seeing the lost children be so near and yet so far from the people they loved, found one more place to crack. 'What's wrong with Byron? What have you done to him?'

'Stay back!' Gwen shouted, and, unable not to obey her, it seemed, the Helynt stopped their advance. But Cassie and Siân hadn't spent years and centuries doing whatever Gwenhidw told them to do, and they weren't about to start now. Cassie moved closer.

Gwen raised a wooden bracelet, neatly decorated with flashes of iridescent green, in her right hand. She stood over Byron the way a victor might stand over the body of an enemy. 'Stop!' she said.

Cassie faltered. 'What are you doing? Get away from him!'

Gwen crouched and started stroking Byron's hair. He flinched in his sleep and tried to move away, but it was just a reflex. He wasn't able to fight back.

'One moment wearing this,' Gwen said, 'is enough to tear all the years of your life away, turn them into the magic that runs through the walls of this place. Your brother is so full of life. He has so much to live for. His years might revive the blackthorn, might strengthen the derew, for a while at least.'

Cassie couldn't move. Couldn't understand what was happening. Gwen had no pity, no mercy in her. 'But there's no need,' she whispered. Then, louder. 'There's no need! The blackthorn isn't dead. It's growing above ground. Please! You just need to see it, and you'll know. You don't have to do this!'

Siân reached over to Cassie, fumbled for her hand, held on tight. Both of them willing Gwen to put down the bracelet, to leave Byron be.

'I do have to!' Gwen said, angry. 'For nearly two thousand years I've protected the derew. I kept them safe. I waited.'

'Waited for what?' Cassie asked.

Gwen stifled a sob. One of the small group of derew stepped away from its small pack and nuzzled its head against Gwen. She dropped a hand to its head and closed her eyes for a moment.

'Waited for who, Gwen?' It was Twm who spoke. Cassie looked to her right. Twm, with his parents at his shoulder, had moved closer, despite Gwen's instruction. Cassie was surprised to hear tenderness in his voice, even care for Gwen. Had his anger passed?

'The Druids,' Gwen whispered. 'The Druids scattered to the four winds when the Romans came. Their sacred groves were burned. Their temples torn down. They had to hide the derew down under the mountain, where the Romans couldn't reach them. They chose someone to protect them that the Romans would never suspect — a girl.'

'You?' Siân asked. 'You were that girl?'

Gwen wasn't listening. She was lost, it seemed, in her own story. 'They took a gift from the girl, and gave her a bracelet made from the wood of the blackthorn tree that guarded the gate between the two worlds. And the girl waited.'

Gwen was a human, Cassie realised, dumbstruck. Not the queen of the tylwyth teg at all, but just another village girl stolen away from her family. Gwen leaned away from Byron and pressed herself against the dead bark. More derew moved towards Gwen, chittering and bobbing their heads, trying to offer sympathy, Cassie thought.

'The girl waited for the Druids to return,' Gwen whispered. 'Over time the girl forgot the colour of the sky, she forgot the sound of birds and the taste of the wind in summer. She forgot she had ever been a girl. And the blackthorn tree grew bigger than any tree should — well beyond its natural years. And still the Druids didn't come. Then the derew began to grow weak. And the Druids didn't come.

'And then, one day, there was Twm. He crawled down into the earth, curious to see what was there. He was so alive.

He smelled of the wind and the heather on the mountain. His years could keep the derew strong for a while longer, until the Druids returned for us all. So, I used some of the blackthorn's magic.'

'The way the Druids had trapped you,' Siân suggested.

All the Helynt, their ghostly parents, and the derew were still, listening to the story of how they came to be.

'But it didn't last,' Cassie offered. 'Twm's strength didn't last, so you took another child, and another, and another.'

Gwen nodded slowly. 'I kept the derew safe. And I will keep them safe until the Druids come back for us.' Gwen's hand dropped from the derew closest to her. She reached to the ground, to Byron's arm. Her fingers circled his wrist. She lifted the dead weight of it and, with her free hand slipped the wooden bracelet over the very tips of his fingers.

'No!' Cassie shouted.

'Don't! Please,' Siân yelled.

But before Gwen or any of them could move, they heard a terrible sound. A deep *crack* like the bones of the earth breaking. Cassie felt a shower of grit and small stones bounce around her like rain; she heard the moan of rock moving against rock, smelled a sudden bloom of damp earth.

She looked up and saw a gash spreading across the roof of the Thorn Hall. The ceiling was breaking above them all.

# Chapter 39

The ceiling of the cavern was crisscrossed by veins of black — cracks were opening. More dirt showered down. Cassie heard a rumbling sound, like a bus driving too fast down a country lane, like rocks bouncing down a quarry face, like a landslide.

The cavern roof was crumbling.

Below the blackthorn tree, Gwen dropped Byron's bare wrist.

Cassie covered her head with her arms. All around Helynt ducked and tucked themselves up small. Their parents tried, uselessly, to cover the children with their bodies, to shield them from the falling stones. The Helynt cried out as they were bruised and beaten by the debris.

'Get out of the way!' Siân yelled.

Cassie looked up, shielding her eyes, expecting to see chunks of ceiling hurtling towards her.

Instead, she saw blue light plunge down from the cracks, like shafts of unexpected sunlight. Magic. There was more magic breaking through into the Thorn Hall. Then Cassie saw why.

Roots. Tree roots, growing faster than anything she had

ever seen before. They writhed like snakes, their fine hairs crumbling the ground as they grew, breaking through Annwn's magical barrier, which flared bright and wild as it shattered.

It was like the tree growing so quickly in Nain's greenhouse, but this one was below the earth.

Cassie paused. Stunned. She shook dirt from her hair, her face.

Was it Nain's tree?

Could it be?

Nain's house must be right above them on Penyfro Mountain. But could her tree have grown so big, so quickly?

With a crash and a dousing of grit and dust so heavy that her eyes stung and her tongue tasted earth, part of the ceiling fell. The roots of the tree burst through the hole and whipped back, snaking along the ceiling and forming a support. New arches and buttresses of wood grew where once there was stone.

The rain of grit eased a little. The ceiling was stabilising. Most of it was still up above their heads, held in place by the curling roots. In the centre of the root cluster, like a ceiling rose where the light fitting jutted through, was a blackness: a tunnel had opened up.

Then, Cassie saw a torch beam dancing inside the roof tunnel.

'Cassie! Siân!' the yell came from the dark hole in the earth above her head. Her heart fizzed and leaped in her chest at the sound of the voice that she recognised so well.

'Dad? Dad!' Cassie yelled at the full strength of her lungs. 'Daddy, I'm here.'

'Stay still, I'm coming!'

The Helynt were rising to their feet, dusting off the fallen dirt, shaking specks of ceiling from their hair, as, in the centre of the Thorn Hall, a tree root unwound, as though the blackthorn were extending its finger. Holding the root was Dad, like something from a spy movie.

As soon as the root touched the ground, he leaped from it. Cassie launched herself at him. 'Dad! You're here. How did you get here?'

Dad held her hard, lifting her off her feet. He was solid as the earth itself. 'We could see the tree growing, even from the railway line. It seemed to me that if it was growing up, it must be growing down too. I grabbed my spare torch and went to investigate — and here I am! The council aren't going to be happy about that ruddy tree, I can tell you, it's causing chaos up there.'

'Uncle Gareth!' Siân shouted. 'Quick!' Siân pointed to the old blackthorn, where Byron lay, cradled by its roots. Gwenhidw stood over him, the wooden bracelet still in her grasp.

'He mustn't wear that bracelet,' Cassie said urgently. 'It's how this all started. The Druids made Gwenhidw wear one and she's been stuck here ever since.'

Dad gave a firm nod. He understood the seriousness of the situation.

He took a few dancer's steps towards Gwen, his palms held up, so as not to alarm her.

'Stay back!' Gwenhidw shouted. 'I mean it. Stay back.' Her face was contorted: eyes more pupil than iris, mouth strained, even the skin on her cheeks and brows was pulled tight in anger.

Cassie had never seen anyone so fear-filled.

Dad took another step. 'Hush, it's OK,' he said. 'It's OK.'

Gwen clutched the bracelet to her chest. She looked to the small, still derew and the dead tree they rested on. Her stained sleeves were smeared dark with her tears.

'Gwen,' Dad whispered. 'Gwen, that's your name, is it? Nice name. My old Sunday school teacher was called Gwen.'

Cassie and Siân watched, fearful, as Dad moved closer to Gwen, the way someone might move near a wild animal — deliberate, slow, even.

'Well, Gwen, that's my boy you have there. That's Byron. Me and his mam, we love him to the bloody moon and back. He's a right one sometimes, but he's a good boy. Can you hear me, Gwen? Look at me.'

Gwen blinked a few times, her shoulders slumped. 'I can hear you,' she whispered. 'He gave me a gift. He wanted to stay.'

Dad was close enough to reach for her, or grab Byron, if he wanted to. But he went no further. He let Gwen feel whatever it was she was feeling. Stood with her, as she cried.

And, as her tears fell, the ancient blackthorn that had stood in the Thorn Hall for nearly two thousand years, split in two. Its enormous trunk cracked and the hollowness inside, the emptiness at its heart, was revealed. The tree had been dying for a very long time. From the flaking bark something small, something metallic, fell to the earth, bouncing with a tinny sound before lying still. The still-bright metal was curved in an animal shape, but Cassie couldn't tell what it was.

Cassie remembered, suddenly, that she'd noticed something metal pressed into the bark of the tree when she'd climbed it. It had hardly been anything, not worth her notice. But Gwen was staring at it as though it were on fire. She recoiled from it, pained by it, it seemed. Whatever the thing was, it meant something to Gwen.

'What is it?' Dad asked.

'My brooch,' Gwen said. It was hard to tell, from her voice, what she was feeling. She sounded frightened, yes, but relieved too, somehow.

'Is that your gift?' Siân asked. 'Is that what you gave to the Druids?'

Gwen put the bracelet down sharply. She stepped over Byron, moved closer to the small silver brooch on the ground. Her hand hovered over it.

'Take it back,' Twm said softly.

'Take it back,' Bridget added.

'Take it back . . . take it back . . . take it back . . .' The words were repeated by the Helynt all around the hall.

Gwen crouched low to the ground, looking for all the

246

world like a little girl who had paused to watch rain drop into a puddle, or a dandelion grow between paving slabs. Gwen held her fingers out . . . then snapped them back, stood, turned away. 'I can't,' she said. 'I was given this task to do!'

Dad waved Cassie and Siân towards Byron — *Check on him,* the gesture said.

Cassie lunged to her brother's side, not needing a second invitation. His skin was warm. His chest rose and fell regularly. He was alive. Asleep, maybe even in a charmed sleep, but alive.

'Gwen,' Dad said. 'I see you,' he said. 'I see it. I know what you're feeling.'

Gwenhidw frowned at Dad.

'I do,' Dad continued. 'I know it hurts. You were left all alone to do an important job and it was terrifying.'

Gwenhidw's eyes focused on Dad. Held him with her gaze. 'What do you know about me?' Her words should have sounded bold, but instead, they sounded broken.

'They asked too much of you,' Dad said softly. He gestured at the dead tree. 'They asked you to stay in the underworld and guard their way of life, their beliefs, while the world moved on without you. It was too much to ask, but you did it. You should be proud. You should be happy. But you should also stop now. It doesn't have to be this way any more. You're scared. I know. But it's time. You've done enough.'

'I have to do my duty until the Druids come back,' Gwenhidw whispered.

'They were never coming back,' Dad said. 'They could never come back. But that's OK. You don't need them any more.' Dad stepped closer to Gwen.

Cassie held her breath in case Gwen should throw Dad across the cavern with her magic, or the derew should swarm all over and crush him. But they didn't move.

'You can rest,' Dad said. 'It's all right to rest.'

Gwen dropped her head. 'It was my mother's brooch. And my grandmother's before that. It was so beautiful. Shaped like a hare, you know.'

'Take it back,' Dad said, 'if you want to. You can move on, if you want to.'

Gwen bent down, reached for the brooch with both hands and clasped it tightly.

Above her, magic flashed in a burst of blue light.

Cassie shielded her eyes, wincing against the sudden brightness. Once she had blinked away the red and green after-bursts, she could see that there was a new ghostly form in the Hall.

A woman, edged in the same blue aura as the other parents, stood in front of Gwenhidw. The woman wore a loose tunic, her hair tumbled free around her shoulders. She came to rest on the branch, beside Gwen.

The likeness between them was unmistakable.

Cassie watched, waiting for the crushing disappointment

that Gwen would feel when her mother's embrace passed right through her. What would her rage, her anger, look like then?

But that wasn't what happened. The woman smiled at Gwen, who smiled tearfully back. Gwen raised her hand to touch her mother, and Cassie saw that Gwen's hand was shot through with blue light. Gwen's body was fading to become the same shimmering stuff as her mother was made from. Gwen was becoming the magic. Her fingertips reached her mother's face and rested, snow soft, on the surface of her skin.

They were touching each other.

Gwen's mother held out her arms and the shining shape of her daughter fell into them and for the first time in two thousand years, Gwen hugged her mother.

Cassie could see the sobs wracking Gwen's body. She had a lump in her own throat.

Around the room, the Helynt — the village children — too were fading to blue light. Each one of them becoming memory. Each one of them embracing their own families firmly and fiercely for one last time. Cassie couldn't help but cry as she heard the delight, the love as they finally, finally greeted each other.

*My love, my boy, my sweet girl.*

*Mama, Tad, Daddy!*

And Gwen held up, held strong, by her own mother, stood at the centre of it all.

# Chapter 40

The Helynt were falling out of focus, even as Cassie watched. The longer and stronger they were held by their families, the harder it was to see where one person ended and the next began. They were blurring somehow. Twm smiled and smiled at his mother as they both faded into the arms of his father. His eyes closed, so peacefully, before their shapes were gone altogether.

'Gwen!' Siân shouted. 'What about Byron? How do we get him back?'

Byron hadn't moved at all, he barely seemed to be breathing. But Gwen didn't look Siân's way. She only had eyes for her own mother.

'Gwen!' Cassie insisted.

'Here,' a voice said. To her right stood Alun Wyn. His pale face was streaked with dirt, even his eyelashes looked dusty. He glowed a soft blue, but was still mostly there. He held something in his hand, offering it to Cassie. Taid's watch.

'I know that's what he gave Gwen. I remember. I fetched it from the Tanglement. He should have it back.'

Cassie nodded, took it gently by its black leather strap. She turned it over. *Dylan Thorn, loved always,* it said on the back. Nain had had it inscribed.

'There's a boy called Dylan Thorn in my class at school,' Alun Wyn said. 'He plays rugby. He's good.'

'Yes,' Cassie said. 'I know him.'

Alun Wyn beamed, his smile as warm as sunshine. And then, magic flowed over, around, through him and the boy was gone.

All of the children were gone. The derew, Gwen, the parents. All gone.

It was just Cassie, Siân, Dad and Byron left with the split body of the dead blackthorn and the quickly fading light.

Siân snapped on Dad's torch. 'Let's get out of here.'

'You'd better lead the way,' Dad said.

Cassie fastened the watch on Byron's wrist. As Dad carried him, slung over his shoulder like a sack of coal, Byron's eyes fluttered open.

'What's going on?' he asked.

'Nothing,' Cassie answered, 'no thanks to you.'

They all stumbled out of the railway tunnel together. Dad, Cassie, Siân, Byron. The air was frost-cold, the stars were pricks of ice in the navy canopy above them. But it tasted clean and alive. Then, Mam and Nain were upon them, cooing and fussing over Byron, and Dad said, 'Come on, let's get this lot home.'

From behind her, Cassie heard a gentle *thump* and knew that the way into Annwn was closed, the invitation to enter withdrawn.

She followed Dad along the railway path, and didn't glance back.

# Chapter 41

'Do you think we'll see her again?' Cassie asked Byron.

They were in the back garden. Cassie held the big plastic laundry basket while Byron reached up to unpeg shirts and sheets and pillowcases from the line. He slam-dunked them into the waiting basket and made a crowd-cheering sound: Y*essssss!*

'Yeah, but do you though?' Cassie insisted. It had been two days since she had heard Annwn close behind them and Dad had carried Byron out of the tunnel. Byron had woken up, then slept for ages, then eaten three bowls of cereal and a cheese and crisp butty, and Mam had smiled at him like a Cheshire cat while he did it. 'Byron!' Cassie insisted. 'Do you think we'll see Gwen again?'

Byron lifted the full basket out of her hands. 'No. I don't think so. Before, I could sort of feel her there, under the mountain. Now I can't.'

'What do you feel?' Cassie asked. Byron hadn't really talked about his time in Annwn.

'A bit stupid,' he said with a grin. 'Thanks for coming to get me.'

Cassie shrugged, as though it was absolutely no big deal and she wasn't going to insist on *always* having the good scooter — which she most definitely was.

'Kids,' Dad said, standing at the back door, 'I was thinking of going for a walk up the mountain, to clear the cobwebs. Do you want to come?'

Cassie flashed a glance at Byron. He was on the cusp of saying no. She could see it in the frown around his eyes, the hunching of his shoulders. Then, he relaxed. 'Yeah, OK. Sounds good. I'll just take this inside.'

'Me too?' Cassie asked.

'Yes, of course. Your auntie Sara's with your mam, at Nain's. She's got presents from Fuerteventura to hand out. Perhaps we can persuade them all to come for a jaunt up Penyfro Mountain?'

'Siân would like that, I think,' Cassie said. She dashed inside to grab her coat. Her sensible winter one, not her denim jacket — it would be cold and windy now autumn was nearly done.

Not that you would know it.

The strangest thing had happened to Penyfro Mountain after they had come out of the tunnel. Up on the heather-strewn moor, the village had suddenly acquired a new forest. Tangled blackthorn, frothing elder and slender stands of beech had grown up overnight.

And it wasn't just trees that had made their home there. The villagers had reported seeing fat beetles, three times the size of regular beetles, shining jewel-coloured and clumsy as bumblebees, flying between the new growth.

The derew were making their home on the mountain again.

Cassie didn't know what it meant, whether that was good or bad. It was just new, just different. Or rather, just really, really old and something they'd have to get used to. The tree in Nain's greenhouse – *on* Nain's greenhouse – had shrunk down to a more regular size. It was happy enough as a mature blackthorn. Nain said she was looking forward to the sloe gin next year.

Once they were ready, Dad opened the front door and they all bundled out. Dad laughed at something Byron said. Byron grinned back, happy to make Dad happy.

'Look!' Cassie said.

But Dad and Byron were already walking towards Nain's, so they didn't see what Cassie saw.

At Mrs Owens-across-the-way, there was someone standing on the doorstep. He was an old man, but not so old that he couldn't stand up straight as he pressed the doorbell.

There was something about him that made Cassie stay and watch. The familiar angle of his chin, maybe, or the way he held his shoulders.

The door opened.

And, as Cassie had somehow known she would, Mrs Owens gasped. She reached out and touched the old man's face, a face she hadn't seen for far too long. Then she stepped aside and let him in.

'Cassie! Cassandra Delyth Thorn, stop dawdling!' Dad shouted.

So Cassie ran to where her Dad and her brother waited, and headed, arm in arm with them both, to see what else had changed that day in Penyfro.

# Acknowledgements

This book was written mostly in lockdown, so first, huge thanks to all the essential workers and medical staff who were, and remain, utterly brilliant. Thanks too to all the storytellers: the novelists, TV writers, filmwriters — we've never needed you more. Jodie, thank you for everything always. Charlie helped me to see what this book was really about; Chloe and Eloise made sure it was fit to be seen in public; Kate made it beautiful. Thank you! And thanks, finally, to family and core crew who kept me as sane as it was possible to be.

# SEASON OF SECRETS

## SALLY NICHOLLS

On a wild and stormy night Molly runs away from her grandparents' house. Her dad has sent her to live there until he Sorts Things Out at home now her mother has passed away. In the howling darkness, Molly sees a desperate figure running for his life from a terrifying midnight hunt. But who is he? Why has he come? And can he heal her heartbreak?

'A stand-out story . . . exciting [and] profound'
**Guardian**

'A wonderful, evocative, lively book'
**Literary Review**

9781839130465

# The Secret of Splint Hall

## KATIE COTTON

1945. War has ended, but for sisters Isobel and Flora, the struggles continue. They've lost their father and had their home destroyed in a bombing raid, and now they must go to live with their aunt and her awful husband Mr Godfrey in their ancestral home, Splint Hall. From the moment of their arrival it seems that this is a place shrouded in mysteries and secrets. As the girls begin to unearth an ancient myth and family secret, the adventure of a lifetime begins.

9781839131967

# EVERNIGHT

## ROSS MACKENZIE

### THE EVERNIGHT
### HAS BEEN UNLEASHED ...

As far back as she can remember, orphan Larabelle Fox has
scraped together a living treasure-hunting in the sewers. In
a city where emotionless White Witches march through the
streets and fear of Hag magic is rife, Lara keeps her head
down. But when she stumbles upon a mysterious little box in
the sewers, Lara finds herself catapulted into a world of wild
magic – facing adventure, mortal danger and a man who
casts no shadow.

'Epic good-versus-evil fantasy'
*Guardian*

'Beautifully cinematic, *Evernight*
is a spellbinding tale'
*The Scotsman*

# LIGHTNING MARY

## ANTHEA SIMMONS

### WINNER OF THE MIDDLE GRADE STEAM BOOK PRIZE

One stormy night, a group of villagers are struck by lightning.
The only survivor is a baby – Mary Anning. From that moment
on, a spark is lit within her.

Growing up poor but proud on the windswept Dorset coast,
Mary faces danger to bring back valuable fossils to help feed
her family. But tragedy and despair is never far away.

Mary must depend upon her unique
courage and knowledge to fulfil
her dream of becoming a scientist
in a time when girls have no
opportunities. What will happen
when she makes her greatest
discovery of all . . . ?

9781783448296

# WHEN THE SKY FALLS

## PHIL EARLE

1941. War is raging. And one angry boy has been sent to the city, where bombers rule the skies. There, Joseph will live with Mrs F, a gruff woman with no fondness for children. Her only loves are the rundown zoo she owns and its mighty silverback gorilla, Adonis. As the weeks pass, bonds deepen and secrets are revealed, but if the bombers set Adonis rampaging free, will either of them be able to end the life of the one thing they truly love?

'A magnificent story . . .
It deserves every prize going'
**Philip Pullman**

'An extraordinary story with historical and family truth at its heart, that tells us as much about the present as the past. Deeply felt, movingly written, a remarkable achievement'
**Michael Morpurgo**

9781783449651